JOHN CRANNA was born in ~~Momona~~ in ~~1954~~ and grew up in the Waikato. He spent a number of years in London, and now lives in Auckland.

His short stories have been published in Britain and New Zealand, and in the international anthology *Best Short Stories 1987*. Five of the stories in this collection have been prize-winners or finalists in national awards and another has won an international prize.

John Cranna was awarded the 1989 New Zealand Literary Fund Writing Bursary.

VISITORS

JOHN CRANNA

With best wishes

John Cranna

11. 10. 90

PACIFIC WRITERS SERIES

Published by Heinemann Reed,
a division of Octopus Publishing Group (NZ) Ltd,
39 Rawene Road, Birkenhead, Auckland.
Associated companies, branches and representatives
throughout the world.

ISBN 0 7900 0050 4
© 1989 John Cranna
First published 1989
Printed in Australia by
Australian Print Group, Maryborough, Vic.
'Leti' and 'Huia and the Angry Earth' have been published
previously in the *Listener*; 'Visitors' in *Stand* (UK) and *Best
Short Stories 1987* (William Heinemann, London);
'Archaeology' in *Insight*; 'Soft Targets' by the Te Awamutu
Festival Society; and 'Cast in Glass' in the *Dominion Sunday
Times*.

The author wishes to acknowledge the kind assistance of the
New Zealand Literary Fund.

To Verna

CONTENTS

VISITORS

MY GRANDFATHER WAS a large man with a strong laugh who grew pomegranates for pleasure, but for reasons that only gradually became clear to me, and certainly were not clear to him, it was felt necessary from time to time to strap him to a bed and apply electric shocks to his head.

When I saw him after his treatment he had difficulty in recognising me, so I stood at his side for a while, repeating my name until the dullness had gone from his china-blue eyes. Although I was only fifteen, I was careful to arrange my face into a mask of apologetic innocence, in fear that he would begin to link my appearance with the treatment he was receiving. When the Pale Suits had gone away he would get up slowly and go out into the garden, where he would walk for a time, occasionally stopping at one of his fruit trees to touch the skin of a pomegranate that had hung there all summer, as though extracting its smooth permanence from the wreckage that had been made of his immediate past.

My grandfather had travelled in the time when this was still possible, and had collected musical instruments from around the Pacific. They stood in the dim corners of the house, or hung on the walls, a great Javanese gamelan in the hallway, and a Chilean lute on a shelf above. In the long afternoons when our visitors worked on my grandfather in the front room, I could hear the instruments in their other lives singing to me. The gamelan I knew well; it sat on the edge of a clearing in the jungles of Java, played by smooth-faced boys, its heavy sound mingling with the trees and the soil. The sound was very clear to me; it lodged in my chest as a kind of ecstasy, and it would only fade when the surge of voices from the front of the house told me that the men had finished with my grandfather. They went then to the kitchen and spoke to my mother, although I

1

could never hear what they said to her. I watched from a window as they walked down the drive, two men in pale suits, one of them carrying an aluminium case, which was laid carefully in the back of the waiting vehicle.

The house and the garden were too large for the three of us who lived there, we had unused rooms, some still locked and containing the possessions of members of the family whose whereabouts were no longer discussed. On one side of the long hall that ran through the house my grandfather and I had our rooms, and on the other, at the furthest end of the hall, was my mother's room, a sanctum that no one was allowed to enter. My mother was a graceful person who moved about the house without ever seeming to touch it, and who each afternoon following lunch would brush my cheek with the lightest of kisses, before retiring to her room for the remainder of the day. After she had gone the long hall held a trace of her perfume, lingering there amongst the instruments, as though the house was reluctant to concede her departure.

At the edge of the orchard my grandfather sat and watched his pomegranates ripen, indifferent to passing showers. In a murmur that carried across the lawn to the house, he spoke endlessly of his years travelling the Pacific in search of instruments for his collection, struggling to prevent the treatment he was receiving from unravelling the thread of his memory forever. I sat beside him on the grass and tried to follow the path of his reminiscences. From Java and the jungles of Indochina it would lead suddenly east to Mexico, then south to the deserts of Chile, before veering west again to the island chains of Micronesia. A story that began in Djakarta might end in Santiago without his being aware that the location had changed, and fragments and characters from one tale would find their way into others, so that his monologues were jigsaws of confusion that held me entranced for hours, but which I could never fully understand.

Some things, however, were clear to me. He had always stayed among the ordinary people, whether it was in the shanty towns of the great cities or in the small, poor towns of the

2

interior. He was obviously welcome in these places, and because of his enthusiasm for the music of the people, instruments would be produced and impromptu concerts arranged. He was often invited to join in the music-making and in this way he became a competent performer on dozens of the instruments he had collected. I could only dimly recall the times from my childhood when he performed for the family in the front room, but I have a clear memory of his large figure stooped forward slightly, playing a lute made from the shell of an armadillo, and holding it so carefully in his arms that he might have been cradling the shell of a massive rare egg. The lute, which was from Chile, now rested in the hallway, where it had remained untouched for many years.

One of my grandfather's remaining clear memories was of his time in Chile and he told me of the year he had spent there in the northern deserts, studying the ancient music of the Atacameno Indians. The language of their songs, he said, was so old that the performers did not understand it themselves, and he described the strange sound of the great side-blown trumpets that accompanied the performance. He had lived in the home of one of these musicians and he spoke of the stark beauty of the deserts and of the resilience of the people who had lived there since the dawn of time. One day, as we sat in the orchard, he told me with surprise in his voice that he had never been happier than when he was with the Atacameno, but when I asked him why he had left, his eyes dulled and his story slid off once more into confusion.

The men in pale suits were visiting twice a week now, and as I sat there beneath the fruit trees, I heard the quiet sound of their vehicle pulling up at the bottom of the drive. My grandfather fell silent at their footsteps on the gravel, and was suddenly very still in his chair. We could hear the Pale Suits talking with my mother, and then her breathless voice calling to us across the lawn. My grandfather got up and walked slowly towards the house, where our visitors would now be waiting for him in the front room. I waited for a while, then went into the hall and sat there in the gloom amongst the dead instruments. I concentrated very hard, until the loudest sound I could hear was the steady beat of the blood in my ears, then softly, across a great distance, I heard the strains of the lute singing in an Atacameno village, and the music grew stronger and more clear, until I was there among the scatter of low huts, listening to the lute as it cut the thin air of the desert. I saw my grandfather, dressed in the clothes of the Indians, working with them in their carefully irrigated fields on the desert's edge, and returning each night to study their ancient music in the household of a master musician. I saw him crouched by an oil lamp, taking down the music of an evening performance in his notebook, and writing out the unknown language that was used in the ritual songs of fertility and death. And then the lute began to sing of strange Indian tribes my grandfather had never mentioned, the Aymara and the Pehuenche; it sang of their languages, of their music, of the rich collection of myth that held together their pasts, and it sang of their struggle against the lethal promises of a new order that had come recently to their land. I was so absorbed by the tales of the lute that I almost missed the babble of voices from the front of the house that signalled the end of my grandfather's session, but the moment the Pale Suits opened the door into the hall, the lute fell silent again.

When the men were in the kitchen, speaking in their sing-song voices with my mother, I went in to see my grandfather. He lay on the bed, the straps loosened at his sides, staring up at the ceiling with unblinking eyes. An acrid smell hung in the room, and a circular stain lay around him on the sheet. I stood there for a while, listening as the kitchen door closed and our visitors' footsteps receded on the drive. I watched the stain spread out across the bed, and thought, They've embalmed him and the fluid is already beginning to leak out. His body seemed a long way off, as though it was withdrawing into the angles of the room, and I felt a sensation of falling. I put a hand out to the wall, and as I did so my grandfather turned his head to look at me, his face blank and his eyes empty of all life. He made a weak gesture with one hand. 'They're very kind to take so much trouble with me. I feel I should be more grateful . . . ' I had

4

never spoken to him about his treatment before, and now, hesitantly, I asked what they had decided was wrong. He frowned, as though trying to remember a complicated diagnosis that had once been fully explained, but eventually he shook his head and lay back, his eyes fixed once more on the ceiling. Behind me the door opened and my mother came into the room in a cloud of perfume. She opened the curtains with one hand while holding a handkerchief against her face with the other. 'What have you done, father?' she said. 'You know you really can't behave like this in front of our visitors.'

That evening, as though in protest at my grandfather's lack of discretion, she failed to appear for dinner, so the two of us ate alone. Although he had bathed and changed his clothes, a faint odour still hung about him, and when I sat down to eat I found my appetite had gone and I could not bring myself to finish my meal.

It had been six years since my sisters and my father had gone away to the mountains. I was too young to understand at the time, but soon after that the schools closed down and before long the Pale Suits called at our house for the first time. My mother would not allow me to go into the city, so the only Pale Suits I saw on foot were the pair who came to visit my grandfather. At other times I saw them passing the house in their long vehicles, and always they were on the wrong side of the road, driving very fast. When I asked my grandfather about the Pale Suits in their vehicles, he was unable to tell me anything. He was fully occupied, it seemed, with his dissolving past, and the only energy he had left for the present was expended on his orchard. There his pomegranates hung thickly on the trees, the best crop there had been in years, he told me, and the fruit were at the point of cracking from within with their own ripeness.

My grandfather spent many hours in the orchard, inspecting the bark of the trees for disease and the leaves for the first signs of summer blight. Often he would stop and stare at a ripening fruit for a time, touching it with his open palm, before moving on to the next laden tree. The longer his treatment continued, the more important the orchard became to him and sometimes he would call me over to a tree and explain his methods of soil preparation and pruning. It was important, he said, that there was someone to take over the orchard when he could no longer manage it. From the bottom of the orchard I could see the outline of the distant mountains, and I began to watch them more closely, thinking of my sisters and my father, trying to imagine them eating and sleeping somewhere among that jumble of pale shadows.

On the next occasion that the Pale Suits visited, the gamelan sang to me, and it sang from a shanty town on the edge of the great city of Djakarta, the music of its gongs shimmering and dancing in the Javanese dusk. Behind the knot of musicians the shanty town stretched away until it disappeared in the haze of cooking fires. The music of the ensemble was very solemn; it spoke of the land the people had struggled for and lost, of their flight to the city, and of the new poverty they had found there. The steady chime of the gongs reached into the corners of the furthest houses, so that it seemed in the end that the entire shanty town echoed with sadness for a time when better things had been promised, and the promises had come to nothing. As night fell, the music faded into silence, and I saw a small boy, asleep on the dirt floor of a hut, clutching in his arms a perfectly made model of the great gongs my grandfather had spoken of. Although he was fast asleep, he held the gong so tightly to his chest that it was possible to believe it was his only possession in the world. But now that the gamelan had ceased, the shanty town was slipping into shadow, and before long I was back in the gloom of the hall, waiting again for our visitors to emerge, the instruments lifeless shapes around me.

I no longer had the courage to visit my grandfather in his room, so I went out and waited for him by the orchard. Eventually he came across the lawn, moving like a blind man, groping his way to his chair beneath the trees. I watched as he tried to speak, his tongue lolling between thickened lips, and I knew then that if his treatment continued in this way it would eventually silence him altogether. I never thought of discussing

6

any of this with my mother. For some years now she had been so detached that her presence in the house seemed almost accidental. We did not discuss the Pale Suits and my grandfather's treatment because we did not discuss anything of importance. It seemed that some part of her had become too fragile to exist in the world of the Pale Suits, so that she had retreated to the sanctuary of her bedroom, a room whose only concrete reality for me was as the source of the mysterious scents and beautiful clothes she wore.

Then something happened which changed the course of the summer. One evening I looked from my window and saw a glow on the horizon, a glow which flared gradually brighter until it lit up a great section of the central city. At one point I thought I heard the distant sound of explosions. It was nearly dawn before the glow subsided to a dull red. The next day there was increased activity on the road outside, with the long cars of the Pale Suits travelling faster and in greater numbers than I had ever seen. In mid-afternoon there was almost an accident, when a driver approached our bend too fast and had to struggle to keep his vehicle under control. I saw a momentary look of fear on the face of the Pale Suit at the wheel, a look that stayed with me for long afterwards. It had never occurred to me that Pale Suits might be able to experience fear. The activity on the road outside continued into the next day, which was a treatment day for my grandfather, and the two of us sat in the orchard and listened to the steady sound of the passing vehicles. My grandfather was slumped in his chair, watching the drive in silence. Even the most halting reminiscence now seemed beyond him. Flies from the orchard settled on his face and arms and he did not seem to have the strength to wave them away. The hot afternoon stretched out for an age, and to pass the time I counted the vehicles as they took the corner. By dusk I had counted a hundred and forty-two and yet the Pale Suits had still not arrived, so at last we went inside to eat. There was a feeling of unreality about the meal that night, I could not recall the Pale Suits having ever missed a treatment day before.

This feeling continued into the rest of the week as the Pale

Suits still failed to call. Outside the vehicles came and went on the road, sometimes alone, sometimes in great convoys, but none of them pulled up in the drive, and by the end of the following week the Pale Suits had missed five treatment days in all. By now I had begun to notice small changes in my grandfather. He moved among the trees in the orchard more freely, his shoulders were straighter and he no longer trailed the faint smell of urine that once had followed him about the house. Before long his reminiscences began again, and now they were a little easier to follow. Tales that had once baffled me with their shifting locations and broken plots started to hang together, as though a fragile thread had begun to run among the scattered pieces of his memory. Some of his stories stirred in me a strange feeling of recognition, as though I had heard them before but when too young to remember or to properly understand. He spoke of his voyages among the endless atoll chains of Micronesia; he told me of the time he had contracted a rare strain of malaria in the Mariana Islands and of being paralysed by village liquor in Guam. The liquor had been drunk at a celebration to mark his mastery of the rare stomach bow after months of apprenticeship to the leading musician on the island. He had lain in a coma for ten days, and on coming to, had been presented with one of the oldest bows on the island, cut from hibiscus wood and strung with finest pineapple fibre. Through some special reasoning that was never explained to him, his coma had been taken as a sign of exceptional suitability for the instrument.

My grandfather told his stories with a new vigour now. There was no stopping him once he had begun on a tale, as though the long months of his treatment had diverted his memories into a dammed lake of the imagination, and the obstruction that had been holding them back had now been cleared away. Instruments which had lain in dusty corners of the house for years and whose origins had been a mystery to me became suddenly recognisable—I identified the stomach bow from Guam at once. The instrument hung in one of the unused rooms, a length of curved wood with a split gourd half-way down its length. My grandfather explained that the gourd was placed against the musician's stomach to amplify the vibrations of the fibre string. From his tales I also identified a shawm from Guatemala, a nose flute from Truk and a log drum from the Philippines.

We would sit in the orchard until after dusk, the trees turning to dim shapes around us, the line of distant mountains catching the last of the light, as my grandfather exercised his returning memory and the fruit flies gathered in clouds above our heads. It was very peaceful there in the orchard, the vehicles on the road outside were another world away, and I began to believe that the Pale Suits had bypassed us, that we no longer had any place in their scheme of things. We had come to a silent agreement not to discuss this, however, for fear that we might alter some delicate balance of invisible forces that was keeping them away.

My mother was unaffected by the absence of the Pale Suits. She came and went in the house in the way that she had always done, appearing in the morning and for meals and retiring to her room for the rest of the day. The house, however, had changed. The windows now let in more light, the dust on the floor did not seem so thick, and the doorways of the unused rooms no longer gaped like mouths onto the hallway. The house was breathing again. I could sense the sweeter air moving among the rooms, and although the instruments were no longer singing to me, they rested more easily in their corners and on their shelves. I felt sometimes that the instruments were beginning to replace my sisters and my father, and I thought of them as more real in some ways than those distant members of my family who had gone away to the mountains so many years before.

In the orchard my grandfather's pomegranates had reached their full maturity, and the branches of the trees bent almost to the ground with the weight of the fruit. The day had come to taste the ·first of the fruit and we decided to hold a small celebration to mark the occasion. We set up a table under the trees and spread it with a white cloth. My grandfather laid out two plates and a cutting board, and I hunted through the drawers until I found the sharpest knife in the kitchen. We knew which of the pomegranates we would choose; we had been watching it for weeks. It hung on a tree near the bottom of the orchard, perfectly formed and with an unmarked skin of deep crimson. My grandfather took the fruit from the tree, placed it in the middle of the cutting board, and we sat down facing each other across the table. We had agreed that I would carve the pomegranate and he would be the first to taste its flesh. When I cut into the fruit I thought that I had never seen a brighter splash of red, and the juice ran in rivulets across the board and stained the white of the table-cloth. My grandfather lifted the pomegranate to his mouth and bit into the flesh, his hands trembling a little as they always did when he ate. I was watching the pleasure spread across his face, when a movement in the direction of the house caught my eye. At the edge of the orchard, standing very still and watching us intently, was a Pale Suit. My grandfather was so engrossed in the fruit that he did not see the expression on my face, he went on eating the pomegranate until he had finished it, while I sat there across the table from him, unable to take my eyes from the stain of the juice on the white table-cloth.

When they had gone inside with my grandfather, I dragged the table around the house and placed it under the windows of the front room. By standing on the table I could reach the level of the window, and although the curtains were drawn, I found that by positioning the table carefully I was able to see a part of the room. At first I could not pick out any details, but as my eyes began to adjust I made out my grandfather's feet on the end of the bed, shoeless and still. Beyond his feet something winked in the gloom of the room, and after a while I realised that it was the light catching the turning reels of a tape machine. I stood there, mesmerised by the reels, my face against the window, and I might still have been there when the curtains were thrown back, if a pale shape had not moved between the machine and the window and broken into my trance.

I carried the table back to the orchard, and set out the cloth and plates as we had left them. Then I went inside to where the stomach bow hung on the wall. I concentrated on the instrument, listening for the hum of its fibre string. Nothing disturbed the quiet of the room. I tried again, straining into the silence, searching for the echo of the distant atolls, and knowing now that it was more important than ever to communicate with the instruments. But the bow would not sing to me; it remained mute and still on its hook on the wall, and I realised then that in my weeks away from the instruments I had lost my old intimacy with them, and I did not know how I was going to close the gap that now separated us. I thought of the pale shapes moving in the gloom, of the turning reels of the tape machine, of the other, unseen contents of the aluminium case that our visitors always brought with them. And I thought about the change that had come over them while they had been away. The Pale Suits had been impassive before; they had come and gone without showing any sign of emotion in their work. But there was something different about them now, a new tension, as though a deep anger lay behind their bland faces. Our visitors were in the front room for longer than I could ever recall, and eventually, exhausted by the knowledge of their return and by my attempts to rouse the instruments, I fell asleep on the floor of the unused room. Much later I seemed to hear the sound of my mother calling, and because she was calling something that was strange to me I could not decide whether I was dreaming. I lay still, and after a long pause I heard her voice again and realised that I was awake and that she was calling to my grandfather in the orchard. I got up and went outside to where the evening light had begun to illuminate the back garden. When I saw the orchard I stopped. Not a single pomegranate remained on the trees. In the middle of the orchard, swaying slightly on his feet, was my grandfather, and around him in all directions lay the remains of the crop of pomegranates. In his hands he held a heavy stick, and his shoes were crusted and stained from trampling the fruit as they lay on the ground. He was squinting into the trees, inspecting each in turn to make sure that he had not missed any of the fruit, and then he threw down the stick and

11

walked past me towards the drive. He stumbled a little, regained his balance and went off down the drive like a blind man, leaving behind him in the gravel a trail of seeds and red pulp. I saw my mother, pale and motionless, watching us from the porch. She seemed to be looking past the wreckage of the orchard to the mountains beyond, and I knew then that she was thinking of the others, but I could not tell from her face whether she believed we would ever see them again. Then she turned and went back into the house. My grandfather was nearly at the road now and I ran after him down the drive. Although the traffic had fallen off a little in recent days, the road was busy, and the great vehicles of the Pale Suits still came and went at speed. I had almost reached the bottom of the drive when my grandfather crossed the pavement and went out onto the road. A vehicle that had just rounded the corner made a wide arc to avoid him, its horn blaring and its tyres crabbing on the asphalt. My grandfather followed it with vacant eyes as it pulled to a halt further down the road. The driver looked back at us through his rear window. By now I had my grandfather by the elbow and was leading him to the pavement. I raised an arm to the driver in the hope that he would drive on. As I led my grandfather back up the drive, I heard the vehicle pulling away into the stream of traffic. Back at the house my grandfather sat in the kitchen looking into space. He did not move or speak for several hours, and eventually I had to lead him like a sleep-walker to his bed.

As though making up for lost time the Pale Suits returned the next day and on this occasion they brought their vehicle to the top of the drive. When they got out I saw why. On the back seat, in place of the usual case, there was a much larger case made of the same bright aluminium and heavy enough to need both of the men to lift it. They were too concerned with getting the case into the house to notice the condition of the orchard. They carried the case down the passage and past the gamelan to the front room, and as they did so I imagined I heard the low chime of a gong, as though the instrument had been brushed in passing. My grandfather sat in the kitchen, watching the Pale Suits come and go, his blue eyes sharp and feverish. When the front room was ready the Pale Suits came into the kitchen and waited for my grandfather to get up. He remained in his chair, his arms limp before him on the table. The three of them seemed to be there an age, the men standing silent by the door and my grandfather motionless in his chair.

At last he got to his feet and went out into the hall, and I knew then that his resistance was over, that his last defence lay in the wreckage of the orchard and that the Pale Suits would now be able to do with him what they wished. When the door to the front room had closed behind them the house became very quiet and I tasted the stale air moving once more through the unused rooms, ebbing and flowing among the inert instruments. Then from the hallway I heard the chime of the gamelan, and as I listened it came once more, a low echo on the dead air. The instruments were waking again, and they had not waited for me to try to reach them first. The chime of the gamelan was solemn and regular now, welling up through the house like a heartbeat, until I could feel it through the soles of my feet and sense its heavy pulse in the pit of my belly. I saw again the shanty towns of Djakarta, the smoke haze low over the huts, and my grandfather sitting cross-legged in the circle of gamelan players; and then through the sound of the gamelan like a sharpened blade came the pure tone of the lute, singing from the deserts of Chile, telling of the ancient music that anchored the past of the people against the shifting sands of the desert. And now other instruments were waking and crowding in on the lute; I heard the sigh of the Guatemalan shawm and the rapid beat of the Filipino log drum. Instruments that had never sung before were breaking their years of silence, emerging from their dusty corners of the house for the first time in order to jostle for place in a chaotic rising choir. The air around me was alive with rhythms that broke in on other rhythms, with melodies that surfaced briefly before being drowned by the surge of some new voice joining the chorus, as instruments struggled to find their true voices after years of disuse. Slowly the milling sounds began to take on some order, the instruments were beginning to complement each other, as though fumbling their way towards a common voice. And then they began to sing in concert, sometimes one taking the lead, sometimes another. They sang of the howl of the typhoon in the tin roofs of the great shanty towns of the East, of the blinding rains and steaming heat; they sang of the harsh lives of the shanty town dwellers and of the peasant farmers on their meagre plots of land. I heard then of the hopes of the people for another life, of their struggle to make a new, better order from the old . . . and suddenly the music of the instruments grew dark and discordant, and the gamelan sang of blood on the grass of the teak forests of Java, the lute spoke of burning huts in the Chilean deserts, and the drum beat out the rap of midnight fists on the doors of Filipino slums.

And like shadows appearing in the cities and in the countryside, I saw men in pale clothing who emerged from the dusk, who stood on street corners and listened in market-places, who went quietly among the people with their soft, sing-song voices, watching and waiting, and who moved when they were ready with deadly swiftness to still the struggles of the poor. I knew then as the dark chords of the music swirled around me that my grandfather had been touched by these things, that his life of travel among the peoples of the Pacific, the secrets he had learnt from them, the music he loved and its sacred place at the heart of their cultures—all this had eventually led him to the dim front room of his own house, where the pale figures of our visitors attended him on a urine-soaked bed, while a lifetime's knowledge slipped through his mind like water through sand.

At that moment the chorus of instruments stopped abruptly and I heard the door of the front room burst open and the sound of feet in the hall. The Pale Suits stood in the doorway, looking about them at the silent instruments. One of the men wore gloves of pale rubber that came half-way up to his elbows. The Pale Suit with the gloves went over to the stomach bow and gently plucked its fibre string. The instrument gave out a low, dull sound, as though it had hung there untuned and unplayed for twenty years. He listened as the note faded into the corners of the room, watching me closely as he did so. 'A young musician,' he said. 'Following in the footsteps of his grandfather.' The Pale

Suit walked among the instruments, sometimes running a gloved finger across a dusty body or plucking a slack string. When he had finished his inspection he stood once more in the doorway with the other man, gazing thoughtfully around the room. Then he turned and the two of them went back down the hall to the front room.

Later I sat in the chair at the edge of the ruined orchard and watched the Pale Suits load the instruments into their vehicle. First they packed the gamelan, after dismantling it into its various pieces, and then added the stomach bow, the lute, and the Filipino log drum. When they had stripped the house of the last of its instruments they climbed into the vehicle, backed slowly down the drive and moved off in the direction of the city.

I set off for the mountains that night; travelling only by darkness and avoiding the roads, I estimated that it would take me ten days to reach them. I did not know how I would find my sisters and my father when I got there, or even whether they were still alive, but I knew that I could not stay to watch the final decline of the house. I saw it then as the Pale Suits would eventually leave it, gutted and open to the weather. I saw the wind lifting the iron of the roof, the rain beating through open windows onto the floor . . . I saw my grandfather wandering through its empty rooms and I saw him going out to sit by a blackened orchard overgrown with weeds, freed at last of the intolerable burden of his memories.

LETI

HIGH OVER THE Pacific they offer us a large sum of money to get off the plane. Neil, a Californian who has befriended me in the San Francisco departure lounge, is keen to accept the offer and is trying to persuade me to join him. We are about to stop in American Samoa for refuelling, and on the island wait a group of tourists for whom, due to an administrative error, there are no onward seats. Although the island is presented in the airline brochures as a tropical paradise, it is known that the Americans are very keen to leave. A steward, in a worried voice, raises the possibility of expensive legal action against his company. He assures us that our food and accommodation will be provided free of charge until the next flight out in a week.

I suspect that we have been approached because of Neil's appearance, which suggests flexibility of itinerary. He wears a denim jacket, an abalone pendant in one ear, and his long blond hair is tied back behind his head with a leather thong. Neil represents the tail-end of a minor exodus from San Francisco that has begun some years earlier. Bay area hippies, aware that an era was drawing to a close, began moving south across the Pacific to New Zealand and Australia, where for a variety of reasons the movement was still alive and well.

'You wanna throw away the chance of a lifetime?' he says incredulously to the plastic tray of chicken normandy that has sat untouched before him since we crossed the equator. I explain that as I have been away for three years I'm keen to get home.

'So after three years, what's one more week?' By the time we land he has persuaded me to take up the offer. We fly over the lagoon in a tropical rainstorm, the big jet bouncing and skimming on the invisible contours of disturbed air, and emerge from the cloud so close to the sea that the wave-lashed reefs are very clear. At the airport an official takes us to a rusted limousine where a quiet Samoan waits at the wheel. We are driven along the coast, passing through groves of coconut palms that run down to black lava beaches. A mist of steam from the recent downpour hangs over the road, and I find myself fighting off a strong sensation of suffocation. Neil has taken the seat beside the taxi-driver and is trying to engage him in conversation. The Samoan drives with one hand on the wheel, his elbow out the window, steering his way skilfully between water-filled pot-holes in the road. In order, it seems, to set up an easy camaraderie between them, Neil takes up a similar position, slouching back in his seat and drumming his fingers on the roof of the car. We pass through a village of thatched *fale*, their storm blinds drawn against the rain, and Neil cranes forward to look.

'Your people still live in those huts?' he asks. The driver swerves to avoid a small boy carrying a suitcase on his shoulder and nods briefly.

'Hey!' says Neil, exultant. 'Just as Gauguin painted it!'

'That was Tahiti,' I say.

'What was?'

'I think Gauguin lived in Tahiti.'

'Bullshit,' says Neil, good-naturedly. He continues his unsuccessful interrogation of the driver until we reach the hotel, where the old limo departs in an arc through the forecourt. In the lobby, five or six middle-aged Americans sit motionless in front of a colour television, while Samoan hotel staff in neat white coats take great care not to cross their line of vision. Our balcony faces out over a beach reserved for hotel guests, which is marked out at each end by a high fence and threatening signs. Across the lagoon stands a line of volcanic peaks, and these peaks, according to our guidebook, form the wall of an immense crater now filled by the sea. The tallest of the mountains is hidden by cloud, and as we watch the cloud thickens, enveloping neighbouring peaks, until it fills the entire lagoon. The rain begins slowly, quickens, then falls with a violence that obliterates all sound, flattening the grass and tearing at the

17

ragged edges of coconut palms. Blood-red hibiscus blossoms, dislodged by the rain, float out into the lagoon.

We are in the hotel bar, waiting for the rain to stop, and Neil is explaining his plans. At some point during his college years he has studied anthropology, and is interested in one particular aspect of Polynesian culture.

'Making it with a Samoan chick should be easy,' he says thoughtfully, turning his glass on the bar. 'They don't have our Anglo-Saxon hang-ups about sex. Balling to them is like eating to us, it's part of their natural daily rhythm. Also, it's an act of friendship, extended to guests.'

'You really believe that?'

'Sure I do. Haven't you heard of Margaret Mead?' he asks.

'I think she was here before the missionaries had made much impact,' I reply. Neil examines his drink with a frown.

'Sure. The missionaries may have screwed things up. But I aim to find the remote parts of the place, where life is still kinda traditional.' I say that I suspect Samoan etiquette is complicated and a minefield for the unwary, but Neil is not listening, he is studying an American couple in their fifties who sit at a table across the room. They are clad in bright Hawaiian shirts and have been arguing in a desultory way over their cocktails since we arrived. On the far side of the lagoon is a tuna-canning factory which interests the husband and which he wishes to visit. His wife is trying to dissuade him; she points out that it is a long walk, and that 'It's sure as hell going to rain on the way.' Eventually they lapse into silence, grey-faced and morose.

'This place gives me the creeps,' says Neil, lowering his voice. 'The people here remind me of decaying cattle.' Maybe the tourists are on a recuperative holiday for the seriously ill, I say, but Neil shakes his head.

'Just Mr and Mrs America on vacation.' Further along the bar sit two Samoan girls speaking rapidly to each other in their own language. One is very striking, she has a low, resonant laugh and as she talks she flicks back her thick, oiled hair. Like many Samoans, both men and women, she wears a red hibiscus flower behind her ear. They too have been watching the American couple, and the striking one drops her jaw in a bovine parody of the discontented husband. Neil grins and winks theatrically, inviting conspiracy against his countrymen; but we have been observed and suddenly the husband is on his feet and walking towards the bar. He stops in front of the girls, swaying a little on his feet. He wears a pair of the high, tooled-leather boots associated with Americans from the Southern states.

'Some little joke you'd like to tell me about?' he asks in a Texan drawl, accentuated by drink. Conversation in the bar has subsided to a murmur. The girl flashes him a smile, revealing very white teeth, then takes the hibiscus flower from her hair and, with an exaggerated flourish, places it behind his ear. To do this she slips off her bar stool, and it becomes clear that she is several inches taller than the American. Disarmed, perhaps intimidated by this statuesque Samoan, he steps back a pace, groping for the flower, and knocks over a bar stool. His humiliation complete, he returns to his table through the quietened bar. Shortly afterwards the couple get up and leave.

At breakfast next morning Neil can't stop talking about the incident.

'The way she handled that jerk,' he says, 'was something else!' He laughs and shakes his head. 'Imagine that. Humiliation at the hands of the natives—in front of your old lady.' After breakfast he says that he is 'Off to do a little field work,' and leaves me with a grin and a wave. Later I walk around the shoreline to the main settlement at the head of the lagoon. There is no hint of cloud on the peaks that surround the bay, and in the clear Pacific light the island is revealed with hallucinatory clarity. Steel containers that have been unloaded from an inter-island trader lie scattered on the quayside, gleaming in the sun.

Past the American naval station is a town of wooden monsoon houses, which seems to occupy its position at the head of the lagoon by temporary invitation, its colonial architecture obscurely at odds with the soft geometry of banana groves, palms and taro patches that cover the hills behind. In the centre of the town I find a fruit market, where a number of listless

19

marketers sit in silence behind long trestle tables. The marketers are all buxom Samoan women, wearing the heavy Mother Hubbard dresses that are the legacy of the missionaries.

Inexplicably, the only fruit on sale are green bananas, piled so high that the long tables bend beneath their weight. There are no customers and the marketers themselves seem paralysed by the midday heat. They watch me as I walk quickly through the market, their oval Polynesian faces expressionless. A thin yellow dog follows me to the outskirts of town, then gives up and turns back. Here the wooden houses have become shacks, their rusted iron roofs humped in imitation of the traditional thatched *fale*. Around them the earth has been churned to mud by the rooting of large pigs, who wander from shack to shack, disappearing inside then re-emerging with an air of casual insolence. A faint smell of open sewers hangs over the street.

Although at last I am free of the shanty town, the smell persists, perhaps now imagined, as I follow a track that winds up into the hills of the interior. Here in the rain forest the air is so thick that it seems to actively resist movement. I stop to rest on a stone bridge, beneath which flows a stream in a bed of blackest lava. There is a deep quiet in the forest, the stream slips by in silence, the only sound is the whisper of sea on the outer reefs. Sitting there submerged in the viridian gloom, I wish suddenly that I had not come to the island, that I had spared myself the spectacle of another declining Polynesian culture. I think of my home, Auckland, the rambling subtropical city that is now the hub of Polynesia; of the Maori pa I knew in my childhood, its strange blend of exuberance and neglect, and of how preferable the pa seems to the town I have just seen. There was nothing of the resistance of the Maori in the faces of the marketers, nothing there at all but hopelessness and lethargy.

As I start back down the track, the first drops of rain break through the vegetation overhead, and by the time I reach the town I am walking through torrential rain, rain that beats tiny hammer blows on my skull and plasters sticky clothes to my body. The market is deserted, its cargo of inedible fruit spirited away. Only the thin yellow dog remains, watchful beneath a dripping stall.

I find Neil in the bar with the Samoan girl, whom he introduces as Leti. Closer up I see that she has violet fingernails and carefully plucked eyebrows. They are discussing the States, and Leti tells us of her collection of Elvis Presley memorabilia, and of her ambition to visit Disneyland, Las Vegas and Miami. From her purse she retrieves a photo of a US marine in uniform, who has promised to show her the real sights of Dickinson, North Dakota, if she should ever visit this, his home town. I expect Neil to be put off by Leti's interest in the more tawdry aspects of the American way of life, but he seems a little drunk, and takes her enthusiasm for his homeland as his cue for a series of rambling tales from the Haight-Ashbury years, which consists largely of the history of one particular communal household, a household riven by drug commerce, personality breakdown and skirmishes between obscure, competing mysticisms. The best of these stories concerns his involvement in an unsuccessful drug-marketing venture. At the time of the venture, nutmeg is rumoured to have strong hallucinogenic properties, a rumour that remains unproven because of the sheer unpalatability of the spice. Neil makes himself very sick confirming these properties, then hits upon the idea of marketing the spice in easily swallowed capsules. Certain of making a killing, he borrows heavily to buy his raw materials: a hundredweight of nutmeg, and a huge number of empty drug capsules from a bankrupt pharmaceuticals firm. For several weeks, working late into the night, Neil laboriously fills the capsules with tweezers and pipette, until at last he is ready to launch his product on the San Francisco underground. But things go terribly wrong. For some reason, possibly related to the collapse of the pharmaceuticals firm, most of the capsules are indigestible, and are passed through the body intact. Confronted by a group of angry customers, Neil suggests taking the pills twice to allow the digestive process another chance, and is badly beaten up for his pains.

21

Leti laughs at the story, she seems impressed by Neil's skill as a story-teller. In fear that Neil has an endless supply of these tales, I suggest that we go for a walk around the bay. The night is very humid, the air carries the scent of rotting vegetation from the interior and the flat odour of fish from the trawlers moored at the head of the bay. We follow the lagoon until we come upon an outcrop of rock, slung low across the beach. Here Neil sprawls on the sand and lights a joint. Illuminated briefly by the glow, Leti's face seems ancient and sad, skin drawn over high cheek-bones, eyes cast down, as though revealed in a moment of unspecific grief. I ask her about her family. She says that they live in a remote village on the other side of the island, and that she stays with an aunt in town. She hasn't seen her family for more than a year. Her voice is distant and she doesn't elaborate. Perhaps, I think, her family disapproves of her presence in *palagi* bars. Neil wants to know more, and eventually gets her to admit to having four older sisters, all still living in the same remote village. At Neil's insistence she describes the village, a scattering of *fale* set on a promontory and bisected by a narrow tidal estuary. Fruit from local plantations and shellfish from the estuary are the staple foods.

Neil moans softly and lights another joint. It is clear that the distant village is becoming the South Seas location of his dreams. He asks Leti about 'child-rearing patterns' and is impressed when she tells him that she spent much of her childhood in the home of a neighbouring relation. His voice, disembodied, emerges from the dark.

'The original primitive commune. Private property doesn't exist, even the kids get passed around. What a way to grow up!' After a silence Leti says that privacy is almost unknown on the island, every event is a public event, there are no secrets.

'That's why I want to leave,' she says. Neil is perplexed.

'What would you want to hide in a place like this?' Leti says nothing. Instead she gets up and walks down to the edge of the lagoon.

When she's gone, I say, 'The location of your favourite pool, how long since you last went to church, your feelings about the presence of Uncle Sam . . . for instance.' Neil sounds aggrieved.

'Don't get heavy, man. I didn't put the missionaries here, or the goddamn naval station.' Out on the reefs the Pacific swell sucks and blows at the coral, yet the water of the lagoon is perfectly still. A squid boat, festooned with lights, glides past us towards the outer channel, a few splintered beads of phosphorescence in its wake. Leti has come up from the beach and is standing near us in the dark.

'You see,' she says slowly, 'Samoa doesn't really . . . exist any more. The pieces of this island don't fit together, or not so they make any sense . . . ' She trails off into silence.

Then Neil shivers and jumps to his feet. 'It's getting cold,' he says. 'Let's go.'

Back at the hotel Neil invites Leti in for a nightcap of duty-free tequila, but after a moment's hesitation she refuses his invitation—her aunt expects her home, she says. I come across Neil in town next morning. He is staring through the window of a hardware shop whose stocks seem to consist solely of enamel basins and plastic clothes pegs. He tells me that the bookshop next door is devoted to hard-core religious literature. 'Like, real Neanderthal stuff, the sort of thing you wouldn't let your kid sister touch.' He adds gloomily, 'You can bet Leti's aunt reads it.'

From a display rack outside the shop I pick up a magazine of the Mormon church, which features an article entitled 'Excommunication of the Fornicators', and is illustrated by a drawing of a half-naked man, his clothes tucked under his arm, fleeing before a mass of dark clouds and jagged lightning. Inside the shop a Samoan boy watches the few customers with a distant, absorbed expression. He laboriously wraps each purchase in brown paper, taking care to stick down the corners with tape, then enters the details of the book in a log on the counter. He has a cluster of sores on the under-side of one arm, which glisten and wink as he wraps the books.

A small girl, a younger sister perhaps, sits on a table at the side of the shop, her liquid eyes fixed on Neil, who is examining a bookshelf with obvious irritation. The little girl, two years old at most, extends a hand towards him, her fingers spread, and utters a sharp, accusing sound. Startled, he turns round, then grinning he holds up a book and addresses her in a serious voice.

'Look, honey, how can you sell this kind of crap?' The boy at the counter comes over swiftly and picks up the infant.

'Leave her alone,' he says. He takes her to the back of the shop, gives her a string of shells to play with and returns to the counter. Out in the street, Neil looks wounded.

'You'd think I'd tried to molest her,' he says. He gazes around him at the dingy shop-fronts and at the monsoon houses with their rusted roofs. 'Let's get out of this goddamn town,' he says.

At a nearby garage we find a van-hire run by a half-cast Samoan. He shows us to a battered Datsun pick-up emblazoned with the words 'Borman Lubrication and Bodies'. Neil is intrigued.

'No relation to *the* Borman,' he says to the Samoan. The man, who is short, muscular and clad in orange overalls, gazes at Neil as though he is a long way off. 'You know,' Neil persists, 'Martin, the Nazi. The one they never caught.' The man continues to stare at Neil and makes no reply. I look at his powerful forearms resting on the bonnet of the pick-up.

'Germans came here last century,' I say. 'With the first colonists.' Neil nods, smiles at the man and climbs into the truck. We take the coast road out of town, through the sporadic palm groves, past the lava beaches, until eventually the road degenerates into a narrow track, pitted with holes and muddy from the rains. Neil is undeterred by the surface, he drives at speed, seldom bothering to avoid the pot-holes and slithering dangerously on the bends. We pass the remains of a van like our own, vivid with rust, picked clean of tyres and upholstery and almost smothered in a predatory tangle of plant life. Eventually we come to a coastal village, where we stop and buy fruit for lunch.

Our presence appears to have no effect on the villagers, the marketer who has sold us the fruit watches us with profound indifference. As we eat, a girl with a leg in plaster limps towards us across the village compound on crutches. The ground is soft and the crutches stick at every step, so that she lurches from side to side like a drunk. Now and then she stops and flails the air with a crutch, as though venting her frustration at her predicament, but when she comes closer I see the cloud of bright tropical flies that hovers over her neck and shoulders. She passes close by without acknowledging us. Somewhere in the village a transistor radio is playing, projecting the breezy voice of an American disc jockey across the compound. The heat is oppressive, the air seems to prickle with static, as though another storm is working its way in off the lagoon. Villagers, half obscured in the deep shade of their *fale*, move about their business with the deliberation of figures in a trance—bending, lifting, crouching on the floors of their open houses. They appear inaccessible, sealed into their domestic routines, and it seems no more sensible to approach them than it would be to approach figures projected onto a distant screen.

The girl on crutches has started on her journey back across the compound. Suddenly she slips, a crutch skids from beneath her and she falls sideways, crying out as her broken leg folds under her body. We run to her, but she pushes us away, speaking furiously in Samoan. I can't tell whether she is directing abuse at us, or cursing in pain. We stand by stupidly while she gets to her feet, arranges her crutches and limps off across the compound. It occurs to me that she looks very much like Leti, the same high, wide cheek-bones and perfect teeth. We are staring after her when a stone thrown from somewhere at the edge of the compound strikes the ground near by. I can make out two figures in the shade of the *fale*, and as I watch, one steps forward into the sunlight, and with the balletic motion of a skilled ball player, throws again. Neil takes the stone in the chest and stumbles backwards. One of the youths cups his hands to his mouth and calls out in an exaggerated American accent, a sardonic parody of the disc jockey's breezy patter.

'Hey, hippie. Go chase some Californian pussy.' We walk backwards towards the pick-up, watching the youths advance across the compound. The radio has been switched off, the village has become a silent amphitheatre, in which only the four of us move. A sea breeze, sticky with salt, chases a scrap of paper across the grass. The youths walk faster now, and still with our backs to the pick-up we do likewise, stumbling on the spongy turf. As we reach the vehicle, a stone strikes the hub-cap with a flat clang, Neil panics, fumbles the ignition key, stalls, starts again and finally accelerates away down the track. I look back to see the youths loping after us, then the rear window turns suddenly opaque as it is struck by a stone. Neil drives at relentless speed for several miles, chewing his lip but saying nothing, then bursts out, 'Fucking animals.'

'They thought you were after the village beauty,' I say. Neil snorts with contempt. 'And you would have been if she hadn't had a broken leg.'

'Whose side are you on?' he says angrily. I shrug.

'Let's start thinking of an explanation for Herr Borman,' I say.

Herr Borman is uninterested in explanations, and makes it very clear that our deposit is only just sufficent to cover the damage to the pick-up. We return to the hotel bar, where Neil starts drinking straight tequilas, feeling his chest from time to time, and saying very little. Then Leti walks in. She wears a simple black dress, and with the usual scarlet hibiscus behind her ear, looks quite stunning. She comments on Neil's pallor and asks him if he is ill. He shakes his head.

'Indigestion,' he says. 'Too much papaya for lunch.' He has come alive at Leti's arrival and insists on buying the drinks. He begins an account of our day in the pick-up, enthusing over the beauty of the island and inventing a friendly welcome in the distant village, which Leti identifies as being very near her home. Apart from our encounter with the youths, Neil omits nothing, his description of the trip is tediously meticulous, and after a while it occurs to me that he is obsessed now with Leti, that he is determined to make a conquest, and that this monologue is an expression of his determination. He is explaining the broken window as a freak accident. ' . . . so this

Nazi screws us for every last cent of our deposit, two hundred bucks for a goddamn rear window.' He gulps down another tequila. Leti smiles.

'Samoans are learning to be good businessmen,' she says. Outside the rain is falling again, and through the window the lights around the lagoon seem to dip and bob in the curtain of water. Neil points a finger at Leti.

'Tomorrow you're coming for a swim,' he announces. 'With me.' Leti starts, as though gripped momentarily by panic, but she says lightly,

'It's forbidden. The beach is for hotel guests only.'

'Then we find another beach,' says Neil.

'I don't like to swim. There are sharks and rays and . . .' With a shrug of her beautiful shoulders she manages to invoke the full range of Pacific submarine terror.

Grinning, Neil says, 'I don't believe it. A Samoan who doesn't like water.' I make some excuse and leave them discussing the dangers of the lagoon. On the long veranda of the hotel I pass the morose American couple, who sit in cane chairs, staring out at the rain as though hypnotised.

I lie on my bed and watch the revolution of the fan in the vaulted ceiling of my *fale*, its shadow in eccentric orbit about my head. There is something about Leti that stirs in me a distant memory, a memory that I cannot isolate and which slips further and further from my grasp. Eventually, to the steady sound of the rain on the grass, I fall asleep. I am woken by Neil throwing himself on his bed.

'She's agreed!' I raise myself on one elbow.

'To what?'

'Tomorrow we're going for a picnic. She's taking me to this place down the coast. Later we'll eat at a little seafood restaurant she knows.' He croons softly to the ceiling ' . . . me and my baby.' Then frowning, he glances at me. 'Hell, you don't mind do you?'

'Of course not.'

'We'd be honoured if you'd have a drink with us, a little later on.'

I laugh. 'You sound as though you're about to announce your engagement.' Neil looks suddenly very serious.

'Uh-uh. You won't catch me doing that trip.' I ask him how he'd changed Leti's mind, and he tells me that as a child she'd been 'traumatised by water', and that once he'd stopped talking about swimming, she'd started to loosen up. He rolls on his side.

'Hey man. Where are we going to put you tomorrow night?'

'I promise I won't interfere in any way.' He regards me anxiously.

'Is that some kind of a joke?' I point out a little testily that it was he who had suggested we share a room in the first place.

'Sure I did. Hell, it's only for one night.' Surprised at the note of pleading in his voice, I say that I'll ask the management if the next room is empty. Neil smiles with relief. 'Tell them you think I'm after your ass,' he says.

It is our last day in American Samoa, and I decide to spend it on the beach myself. Checking first that Neil and Leti have gone in the other direction, I take a path along the shoreline until I come to a small, secluded bay. Here I stop and lie in the sand, watching the land crabs scuttle from the surf as it advances on the beach. A few children paddle in the shallows while their mothers, fully clothed in cotton dresses, swim a little further out. The prism of hot air over the sand distorts the figures so that it is sometimes impossible to distinguish adult from child, boy from girl, and then the prism clears and each figure is picked out against the burning lagoon. A group of young girls has formed around a little boy who totters, stark naked, at the edge of the water, afraid to go any further. Shrieking with laughter, they try to lure him in, but he remains on the beach, his fat little arms spread for balance, until one of the girls takes his wrist and draws him into the sea. The first wave knocks him down, and for a moment he disappears in the foam, then reappears, his face contorted like a monkey's, screaming with rage and fear. He is pulled from the water and carried up the beach, where one of the girls tries to placate him in her arms. The others kneel around the infant and he is passed from one to the other, his screams diminishing as each girl pets and strokes him. He is silent now, and as though administering a final reward, the girl who cradles him bends her neck and firmly kisses his tiny penis.

Neil and Leti arrive back late. Neil is pink with sunburn and clearly exhilarated by his day on the beach, though Leti seems a bit subdued. To celebrate our last night on the island, we order expensive cocktails, which are served ice-cold in goblets almost too heavy to lift. Around us the party of American tourists speak in excited undertones, they seem to be relieved at the prospect of leaving the island. I ask Leti when she plans to visit America, and she smiles a taut smile.

'When I am very rich,' she says. It occurs to me that I don't know what work she does, or in fact whether she works at all, and somehow on this our last evening it seems inappropriate to ask. Neil shakes his head.

'You're heading the wrong way, baby. The Moral Majority are gonna make America uninhabitable in a year or two.' He shudders and plunges his cocktail straw into his glass. 'That's if America's still on the map.' I say that right-wing revivalism is on the move in New Zealand as well, which has certain similarities to the American South, and that the part of the country that Neil is heading for is renowned for its insularity and conservatism.

'That's what I like about you. You're so goddamn positive,' he says. A floor show has been arranged for the departing tourists. A boy crouches over a Hawaiian guitar, waiting for the conversation to subside, then begins a sweet, mournful song, pitched in a minor key and sung in Samoan, a song that quickly entrances the audience with its evocation of sadness and loss. There is a loud ovation for the singer when he finishes, and he stands and bows low to the room, then holds his guitar aloft, as though redirecting the applause to an undervalued co-performer. I ask Leti what the song is about, but she shrugs and smiles. 'The words don't make any sense,' she says. The singer has been joined by a small dance band, and after the first

29

number, several of the American couples move towards the dance floor. Neil looks at Leti and raises his eyebrows. 'How about it, baby?' I watch them take the floor—an incongruous pair as they bob among the older, shuffling couples. They arrive back at the table flushed and laughing, and Neil announces his intention to spend all his compensation payment from the airline that evening. He has ninety dollars left.

Some time later he has succeeded; I have trouble focusing and am feeling quite sick, Leti is giggling unpredictably and Neil has his arm draped around her shoulders. He leans forward and glares at me drunkenly.

'Wha's matter? Wish you hadn't come to this wonnerful place you miserable goddamn Kiwi?' Without waiting for an answer, he continues, 'Hell, I wouldn've missed it for anything. After all,' he grips my wrist, 'you gotta unnerstand how the Third World lives . . . '

I struggle to marshal my thoughts. 'But this is an American . . . '

'And you've gotta unnerstand their women. It's an obligation. A goddamn innernational obligation.' He regards me with bulging, watery eyes, while Leti, her white teeth flashing as she laughs, feeds him glacé cherries impaled on a cocktail stick. I am trying to focus on Leti, on her red, lip-glossed mouth, on her carefully prepared nails, and it seems to me now that her laugh has become a shell, both brittle and opaque, a shell that hides a past so incomprehensible that I am driven to my feet in irrational fear. I remove Neil's fingers, which are still clutching my wrist.

'Going to bed,' I mumble.

I wake, stunned and sober, to a penetrating scream that could have been dreamt. For a time there is nothing but the whisper of surf, and I am drifting back into sleep when a soft, even sound filters into my room, a sound that is ancient in its ambiguity, the sound of approaching orgasm, or alternatively, of deepest despair. I lie still as the sound ebbs and flows through the silent hotel, until it becomes clear that I am listening to sobbing, and that the sound is coming from Neil's room next door. I get into

30

my clothes and go out into the corridor. A bar of light beneath the door dimly illuminates the passage. I knock and wait, but no one comes to the door and the sobbing continues uninterrupted. For a moment I hesitate. Am I intruding on private grief? Will I find Leti inconsolable at the prospect of Neil's departure? Then I recall the scream and softly open the door. Slumped against the far wall, naked except for a wilted hibiscus flower behind his ear, is Neil, sobbing gently. He looks up at me without recognition or curiosity, then drags himself up into a sitting position. He has a lurid scratch mark running from ear lobe to chin, and beside him, on the floor, is a pool of fresh vomit. I notice Leti's black dress, torn and crumpled, in a corner.

'What happened?' Neil stares at me for a long time, struggling, it seems, to accommodate a truth so improbable that it defeats his attempts to speak it.

'Leti,' he whispers, in a voice I have never heard, 'is a boy.'

During the flight to New Zealand, Neil doesn't speak much; he is slumped in his seat and watches, like a man drugged, the unchanging expanse of sea far below. I try to interest him in the geography of his destination, but he does not respond and eventually I give up. Around us the party of tourists, renewed by their departure, speak with enthusiasm about the next stage of their Polynesian tour, and in tones of mild outrage, swap anecdotes about the peculiarities of Samoan cuisine. After several hours of silence, Neil rolls a cigarette and smokes it between pale lips, paging fitfully through the flight magazines provided by the airline. Then as a thin smudge of land appears on the horizon, he grinds his cigarette into the ashtray and bursts out,

'What the hell is going on down here?' By this he seems to mean the South Pacific. 'I mean what happened back there was *sick*. Jesus, it was sick.' With trembling fingers he continues to stab his cigarette into the ashtray, although it is long dead. I try to think of some reply, but I am suddenly overcome by a deep unease, an unease that grows out of three years' absence from my home, the Polynesian capital of the Pacific, a city of extinct volcanoes on an isthmus between two seas, and in that moment

31

I'm certain that I don't want to return. And then Neil is craning at the window, as the big jet banks against a clear blue sky and settles so smoothly towards the runway that it is impossible to say exactly when we have touched the ground.

ACCIDENTS

WHEN I THINK back on Chug's last trip down the shaft, I can't understand why he wasn't more careful. After what had happened on the site that summer, you'd think he'd have suspected something might go wrong. I guess he was used to having things his own way, and that must have blinded him to what was happening around him . . . But all this is in the wrong order. I should tell you about the early days.

I had been on the site for two weeks, the January sun was beating down on us, and the air over the river danced with the heat. Sometimes a breath of wind would filter out of the forest and stir the dust around the cages. The morning, like every morning since I joined the gang, had dragged by in the same exhausting heat. The pliers I was using had brought up a blister, which had burst and was now bleeding. I straightened up, leant against the cage, and stinging drops of sweat trickled into my eyes. For a moment the hillside of forest blurred, then came back into focus. The others had taken their shirts off and their backs were brown and shining with sweat. Behind them, past the finished cages, the excavations for the bridge had left a scar of red earth on the mountainside.

'Smoko time?' I said. Tamati, my partner on the cage, ignored me. There wasn't even a change in his regular movements. He was working towards me from the other end of the cage and a bundle of tie wires stuck out of his back pocket like a tail. He'd already done more than half the cage.

After about a minute I said, 'I've got a blister.' Tamati stopped and turned around. I knew he would react, the blister could mean more work for him. He came over and looked down at the rods I'd tied.

'You want the fucking bridge to fall down?' He bent down and rattled one of my ties, which was loose. The cages were to

33

reinforce the concrete piers of the bridge. 'Watch,' he said. Taking a tie wire, he flipped it round the joint and twisted it tight in a few smooth movements. Because he sometimes wore a singlet in the sun there was a strangely shaped patch of lighter skin on his back. I had never realised that Maoris tan like whites. 'There's a glove in the crane tool-box,' he said as he walked back to his end of the cage.

On the way down to the river I passed Ron, the foreman, and Chug, who were working on another cage. They were almost as dark as Tamati. Before I came to the site I had worked as a night cleaner for two years, and because I never got any fresh air or sunlight, my body was white and pasty, and my back was covered with terrible pimples. That was one of the reasons why I never took my shirt off on site. The other was my chest. I have a deep hollow where my breast-bone should be. A doctor told me that my hands were pressed too hard against my chest in the womb.

As I drew level with the others, Ron said, 'How's it going?'

'OK,' I replied. He nodded vaguely, it wasn't really a question. Ron had a lot on his mind; keeping to the schedule, planning out the day's work and so on. Sometimes he'd stand in the shade and stare at his feet for a long time, smoking a cigarette, while the rest of us worked. All the calculations— tonnes of concrete, metres of steel—he seemed to do in his head. I never saw him use pencil or paper. Ron was quite a good boss, he left me alone most of the time. Even in the first week, when I made a mess of almost everything I did, he just corrected me without getting angry. But he was a crazy driver. Several times on the winding road down from the site he'd nearly finished us all. It surprised me that someone who was so calm could be such a maniac behind the wheel.

Ron usually worked with Chug, the fourth man on the gang. Chug was big with blond hair, and although he was only a couple of years older than me, it was obvious that he thought of himself as some sort of laid-back surfie type. From the way he moved around the site, and the fact that he never wore a shirt, you could tell that he was pretty keen on his own physique.

34

When there was nothing to do, Chug would go and take up his life-saving position on a pile of steel reinforcing. He'd squat there chewing gum and scratching at the blond hairs on his belly. All the time he'd be looking out over the river with a bored expression on his face, as though he was watching over a beach for his next rescue.

I went on towards the river, screwing up my eyes at the glare from the water. When I came to the crane I sat down in the shade of the cab for a rest. The jib of the crane was lowered and the rusty framework lay along the bank like the skeleton of a huge animal. I peeled clods of earth off the cool metal tracks and thought about my first few days on the site. How I'd survived them was a mystery to me. After the cleaning job my body wouldn't adapt to daytime work and every time we stopped for a break I found myself dozing off. We were shifting reinforcing steel down to the site from a stockpile near the road. The long metal rods were flexible and bounced up and down as you walked. I stumbled along behind Tamati, praying that I wouldn't drop my end. If you let go without warning, the impact whipped through the steel and almost jerked the other man's arm off. After a few days of this my muscles were stretched and uncontrollable. And then Tamati went to work on the crane and I was left carrying steel with Chug. The heat seemed even worse then, and my hair was sweaty and falling in my eyes. I couldn't see where I was going, and kept running into stuff lying around the site. When that happened with Tamati he just waited, without saying anything, until I got my grip on the rod again. But not Chug. He would look around with a pained expression on his face, as though I'd deliberately insulted him by cutting my shins open, and carry on regardless. Because of my chest, I sometimes have difficulty breathing, and several times that day I had to stop altogether, gasping and out of breath. The third time it happened Chug went over and spoke to Ron. I knew he was complaining, because Ron glanced across at me. After a while Ron shrugged and turned away. Chug came back in a bad mood. We began work again and he made things as difficult as he could. When we dumped the rod he no longer gave any warning. I lost count of the times my arm was jerked. Chug must have lengthened it by a couple of inches that day.

From where I was sitting by the crane I could see the old wooden bridge downstream. Occasionally a car would cross, and the bridge rattled and shook right down to the piles. Over the summer the water level had dropped so that the bottoms of the piles were exposed like the spindly grey legs of an old man. In a way I was sorry that the new bridge would take its place. I'd seen other bypassed bridges in the hills, abandoned with their snip of road, derelict and covered in weeds. There was a plan of the new bridge in the smoko hut. On paper it looked impressive, but in reality it would be square and ugly, the same as any other concrete bridge.

I climbed onto the crane and searched in the tool-box for the glove. Then I walked slowly back up to the others. Tamati was well into my half of the cage. When I returned he glanced up and then looked at his watch. He had the most bloodshot eyes I'd ever seen. Once I heard Chug joking to Ron about them. He said Tamati must be wanking too much, which wasn't a very good joke because Tamati was married. Chug would never have made the joke to Tamati's face as he didn't have much of a sense of humour. The only time I'd seen him smile was one night when we dropped him at home on the way back into town. His kids came running out to meet him. We were driving away when I caught a glimpse of him grinning as he threw his little girl up into the air.

The glove wasn't helping matters at all. The leather was so stiff with sweat and mud that I couldn't work the pliers properly. I began to snap some of my ties by pulling them too hard. This didn't matter much as no one really bothered to check our work. The construction inspector from town visited the site in my first week, but he was more interested in gossiping with Ron and Chug than inspecting the cages. They stood around laughing and smoking cigarettes while Tamati and I worked. Although Tamati was much more experienced than Chug, it was Chug who talked and joked with the inspector like an old hand. In fact he'd only been on the gang a year. I couldn't tell what

Tamati thought about this. He didn't show his feelings that often.

I was relieved when at last Tamati stood up and stretched.

'Better put the boiler on,' he said. I threw down the glove and pliers and went over to the petrol drum. To make the tea I would pour petrol from the drum into an enamel mug, light the petrol and sit the mug under the water boiler. This time the drum was empty. Ron had forgotten to refill it in town. Tamati pointed to the Landrover.

'Siphon some out of the petrol tank,' he said. I found an old piece of hose, pushed it down into the petrol tank, and lay on the ground next to the mug. When I sucked on the hose nothing happened. I sucked harder and suddenly there was petrol in my mouth. Before I had time to push the hose into the mug I'd swallowed a mouthful of fuel. I began to choke and retch. There was petrol in my lungs and I couldn't breath. I panicked and tried to get to my feet, but I was doubled up by a stomach cramp. I lay on the ground gasping for air, clutching at the gripping pain in my stomach. After a time, breathing became more easy. I got onto my hands and knees and tried to spit out the foul taste of the petrol.

Above me a voice said, 'Thirsty work, building bridges.' Chug was leaning against the cage and grinning. I was shaken by a fit of coughing and then I started to hiccup. I must have looked pretty stupid, kneeling there spitting and hiccuping, with tears streaming down my cheeks. Still grinning, Chug began to imitate me, jerking his body in time to my hiccups. I tried to stifle them, but couldn't. I started to feel desperate.

Between hiccups I manage to croak, 'Shut your face.' Immediately Chug's expression changed. He squatted down in front of me. His blue eyes were hard and vicious.

'Look you little creep,' he said in a quiet voice, 'We were supposed to get a fourth man on this gang, not a gutless wonder.' His finger was an inch from my nose. 'If you can't take the pace, then go push a fucking broom again.' I wanted to spit in his face. Instead I hiccuped. Ron walked past on his way to somewhere else and Chug stood up.

'You alright?' Ron said. I nodded, but he had disappeared around the corner of the smoko hut. I got to my feet, feeling ill and hot, and continued with the tea-making. Tamati stood watching with his hands on his hips. He was looking at me as though I was crazy. For the rest of the day I had a blinding headache, and I kept bringing up a burning liquid tasting of fuel. It's surprising what one mouthful of petrol can do to you. If I'd been in better physical condition it probably wouldn't have affected me like that.

Two days later we finished the last of the cages and moved down to the river to drill the first pier for the bridge. Although the level of the river had dropped, the green water still looked cool and deep. The river ran sluggishly between banks that had become cracked and caked in the heat. According to Ron we were to drive a metal tube into the bank and remove the earth and rock inside. Eventually a reinforcing cage would be lowered down the tube and concrete poured in. My job was to shovel the spoil away from the top of the tube. When the drilling reached water-level the spoil turned to slush, and after a morning's shovelling I was covered in mud. We were in the smoko hut for lunch. The heat from the iron roof made it sticky and uncomfortable. Apart from the occasional creak from the roof, the only sound was the buzzing of flies feeding on a pile of crusts by the rubbish bin. Tamati was sitting on a box of nails, slowly eating the big Maori-bread sandwiches he brought every day. He screwed up a ball of waxed paper in his fist and threw it at the flies. They cleared, then returned to the crusts. As usual Ron and Chug were playing cards at the table. The pack was Chug's and the cards had pictures of nude women on them. Recently Chug hadn't been winning many games. He began to tap the heel of his boot up and down on the floor. He was about to lose again.

As he waited for Ron to play his card he glanced across at me. 'You look like a hori with that mud all over you.' Ron, who had been about to play, stopped with his fingers on the corner of the card. I looked at Tamati. He was no longer eating, and stared at Chug with his bloodshot eyes. Chug turned to him.

38

'Nothing personal, Tama,' he said. After a pause, Tamati began to chew again very slowly. His face was blank and he said nothing. Chug shrugged and turned back to the table. Ron carefully rearranged his cards. A few minutes later Tamati finished his lunch and left the hut. Usually we all left together.

When he'd gone, Chug said, 'A hori's a hori's a hori,' and laughed.

'Shut up,' said Ron. Chug laughed again and began to whistle softly between his teeth. His mood had improved. Since I'd swallowed the petrol I hadn't felt much like eating, and watching Chug made me even less hungry. I wrapped up my sandwiches and lobbed them at the bin, but they hit the rim and skidded under the table. Chug leant over and picked them up.

'How are we going to put any meat on you if you starve yourself?' He laid his cards face down on the table and began to unwrap the parcel with his fingertips, as though he was unwrapping something rotten. I could feel my face growing hot.

'What's this then?' He lifted the corner of a sandwich. 'Ch-rist—celery and walnuts.' He shook his head in pretended wonder and looked to see if Ron was watching. Ron was frowning at his cards.

'Leave them alone,' I said. He ignored me and went on peeling open the sandwiches.

'This one looks a bit poisonous. You sure your Mum's not trying to get rid of you?' I sat on the edge of my seat. There was a tightness behind my eyes that made focusing difficult.

I said, 'Give them back.' He raised his eyebrows in an exaggerated way.

'You just threw them away.' My eyes blurred with tears of anger. I lunged forward to snatch the sandwiches off him and at that moment he tossed them across the room. They hit my chest and scattered around me. I looked down at them, broken and sandy on the wooden floor. There was a piece of mustard-covered ham sticking to the toe of my boot. Then I turned and stumbled out of the hut. As I left, Ron said something to Chug that I didn't hear.

Later in the afternoon the tube ran up against bedrock. A

weight had to be shackled to the crane wire and dropped down the shaft. Blades set in the end of the weight smashed into the bedrock and sent splinters flying up the shaft. After half an hour's pounding the wire was attached to a steel bucket large enough to hold a man, and one of us was lowered to the bottom to dig out the rubble. Most of the space was taken up by the bucket, and there was hardly any room to swing a shovel. It was easier to use your hands. Despite the heat above, it was quite cool down the shaft. There was always a half-metre of icy water in the bottom, and after an hour fumbling for rubble, my arms were numb up to the elbows. Tamati worked the crane and Chug and I took turns at the digging. Because of his size, Chug had much less room to move than I did. From the top of the shaft I watched him struggling with the shovel in the confined space. Now and then his swearing echoed up the shaft as he grazed himself on the rock. When he came to the surface, standing on the full bucket, his elbows were cut and bleeding and he was chewing angrily on his gum.

After a few days, to my surprise, I found I was almost enjoying the work. This was partly because I knew Chug hated it. I learned to ignore the numbness in my arms, and I found that by working at a regular pace I could avoid losing my breath. The shaft was now about ten metres deep, and I felt cut off from the others on the surface. Sometimes a face would appear at the circle of blue above, but usually they'd leave me alone. No sounds from the surface reached me, the crane could have fallen into the river and I wouldn't have known. It was quite peaceful at times, down there in the half darkness, with just the dripping rock and the muddy water sloshing around my feet.

One lunch-time Tamati brought out a book. I could see that Ron and Chug were surprised. No one thought Tamati was the reading type. You could tell that he found the book difficult, because he screwed up his face to concentrate, and he'd only finished one page by the end of the break. The book had black numbers on its spine, and I guessed that it was from the town library. Within a few days there were teacup rings on the cover and the pages were stained with mud and grease. I thought of what the librarian would say when he returned it. As I had nothing to do at lunch-times I watched Tamati's progress. When he'd read three pages he went back to the beginning of the book and started again. For some reason the sight of Tamati reading a book seemed to upset Chug. Sometimes I saw him watching Tamati with a frown on his face.

One afternoon he said, 'Good book, Tama? Plenty of luscious chicks?' Tamati went on reading. The screwed-up expression didn't change. Chug couldn't stand being ignored. Winking at Ron, he said, 'Come on Tama, don't keep all the filthy bits to yourself. Share them with your mates.' There was something different about Tamati now. His expression was the same, but it seemed to have set solid. I could see he'd stopped reading, his eyes were no longer flicking along the page.

Ron noticed too, because he said, 'Leave it, Chug.' He dropped the pack of cards on the table in front of him, 'Your deal.' But Chug wouldn't give up.

He laughed strangely and said, 'Well, we'll just have to find out for ourselves, won't we?' and reached across the table to grab the book. Suddenly Tamati slapped the book shut and brought its edge down with a crack on Chug's wrist.

'Fuck off, cunt,' he said. Chug drew his hand back across the table. His mouth was hanging open and a crinkly piece of gum stuck to his bottom teeth. His eyes were blank and surprised. He looked so stupid, sitting there with his sagging face and the gum stuck to his teeth, that I couldn't stop myself letting out a snort of laughter. Chug turned on me. There were angry patches on his cheeks. Before he could say anything Ron stood up and banged the table with his open hand.

'Alright, that's enough,' he said, 'Let's get some work done.'

Later that afternoon, as it was Friday, I cleaned out the smoko hut. I was sweeping the floor when I saw Tamati's book sticking out of his old green duffle bag. The others were at the river. I pulled it out and began to read. The book was about a Maori leader, some woman who was now dead. She fought to keep Maori land and to stop their customs being stamped out. It was quite interesting. She wouldn't let her people fight in the First

World War. How could she fight for King and Country, she said, when she had no country left. The police came and dragged her men out of their villages, but they still refused to fight. I was interrupted by Ron yelling at me to hurry up. As I went back down to the river I wondered what Chug would have thought of the book. There didn't seem to be any sex in it at all.

The work down the tube had become a lot harder. The deep section of the shaft was to be enlarged, and this had to be done with a jackhammer. Tamati lowered one of us to the correct depth in the bucket, and we would dangle there in space and drill into the rock wall. Balancing with the heavy tool was difficult, as it bucked and jumped like a live animal. To make things worse, the bucket often twisted on the crane wire and bumped against the rock. The walls of the shaft were dripping wet, and the hammer sent up a spray of grit and water which stung my face and hands. Usually I drilled with my eyes shut. Slabs of rock would peel off and tumble into the water in the bottom of the shaft, and several times when this happened I almost dropped the hammer. To begin with, the noise in that narrow tube was unbearable, but after a day or two my hearing dulled and it stopped worrying me. For safety reasons, Tamati had to stay in the crane when one of us was down the shaft. There were long periods when he had nothing to do, so he sat in the yellow cab reading his book. Chug and I did most of the drilling, though occasionally Ron took a turn if he wasn't busy somewhere else on the site. I could see that this arrangement was beginning to upset Chug. Although Tamati was the only one who could drive the crane, Chug seemed to think he should be helping with the drilling. Sometimes Chug would turn and watch Tamati in the cab, his hands on his hips. Before the book incident Chug had more or less ignored Tamati. Now he was looking for chances to have a go at him.

The weather seemed to have become even hotter. For days there hadn't been a cloud in the sky and the heat lay like a blanket on the site. On the hillside the tops of the trees sometimes moved with a light breeze, but at ground level the air was still and scorching. One afternoon I was watching Chug being winched out of the shaft. His blond hair was plastered to his head with water and he had a sour expression on his face. As Tamati swung the jib the bucket caught the top rim of the tube. Chug pitched forward and hit his head on the steel handles of the bucket. When Tamati let him down he walked over to the crane.

'Why did you do that?'

'Do what?' Tamati's voice was level.

'Try to split my bloody skull open.' Tamati shrugged. It was an accident. Chug chewed furiously on his gum. He glared up at Tamati's blank face for a few seconds, then walked away. 'Ignorant black bastard,' he said under his breath. Immediately Tamati leant out the window of the cab.

'What was that?' he shouted. Chug half-turned, hesitated, then continued walking. There was something dangerous about Tamati's flat bloodshot eyes that even Chug couldn't miss. Suddenly Tamati, who was still leaning out of the cab, called after Chug in Maori. It was the first time I had heard him use his language. The words sounded strange and threatening, and for a moment Chug looked uneasy.

Then he turned back to the crane again and shouted, 'Don't talk to me . . . ' but Tamati had put the crane into gear and Chug's words were drowned by the revving engine.

Later that afternoon I was making the tea for smoko when Chug wandered up from the river, squatted in the shade of the smoko hut, and lit a cigarette. Earlier Ron had driven into town for some equipment, and the rest of us had been working in silence for several hours. Chug watched me as I filled the enamel mug from the barrel. Because the barrel was so unwieldy I spilled some of the petrol on the ground. I picked up the mug and walked over to the boiler, and as I did so, Chug casually began to flick lighted matches at me. He held the box on its side and with his thumb and forefinger he flicked the match along the lighting strip. A burning match flew past my elbow and as I jerked away the petrol in the mug slopped over my arm and shirt. I opened my mouth to say something, but the next match ignited the spilled petrol at my feet. A moment later the ground around me was alight. I dropped the mug and it exploded in a ball of blue flame. Suddenly my shirt was on fire, and I beat at it with both arms, but this had no effect so I started to run. I glimpsed Chug's slightly worried face as I sprinted past him towards the river.

I ran down the long slope, past the rusty piles of steel, the mounds of earth and the yellow cab of the crane. There was no pain, just blinding, suffocating heat. I came to the river and plunged off the bank into the cold water, turning over slowly as I sank. I took in great cooling mouthfuls of water. There was a friendliness to the depths of the river that made me feel almost sad to be drifting back to the surface. And then I was in brilliant sunlight, choking and sobbing for air. I floated downriver towards the legs of the old bridge. As I neared the bridge I had to strike out to stop the current dragging me into the centre channel and past the posts. I caught hold of an upright and hugged the slimy green wood. The current rippled around me, tugging gently at my body. I pulled myself up onto a cross support and lay there unable to move.

After a while Tamati appeared on the bank carrying a length of rope over his shoulder. He tied one end to a piece of driftwood and eventually managed to lob it over the cross support. I took hold of the rope and slid back into the river, and Tamati dragged me to the bank. I stood up slowly in the shallows. My lips felt cracked and puffy. Following Tamati's gaze I looked down at my arm. From my wrist to my shoulder the skin had peeled away and the flesh was red and raw, like fresh meat. I touched my head and found that my hair had turned into a black sludge that stuck to my fingers and smelt like rotten eggs. There was still no pain from my arm, and without thinking I pressed the raw flesh. It was quite numb. Tamati grimaced. He looked me straight in the eyes.

'You'll feel that in a couple of hours,' he said.

I sat for a while on the steps of the smoko hut, drying out in the sun. The petrol barrel had caught fire and was still blazing at the edge of the site where the others had rolled it. I watched the column of black smoke rising into the sharp blue sky, my mind completely blank, and waited for Ron to drive me to the clinic in town.

I was off work for a month with the burns. During that time I thought a lot about the site. At first I was a bit feverish, and the burns and the heat on the site became mixed up in my mind. For a while I was convinced that sun had burned me. I stayed in my room with the blinds drawn to keep out the light, leaving it only for meals. When the fever disappeared I began to have nightmares. I dreamt that I ran down the long slope to the river with my shirt on fire and dived off the bank. But because of the drought there was only a trickle of water in the riverbed, and I lay there stunned and burning in a few inches of water, while the others watched me from the bank. One nightmare was repeated every few nights. In it I visited a doctor about the deep pimples on my back. He strapped me face down to his couch and told me in a quiet voice that they would have to be burnt out with petrol. Then he poured purple liquid from a bottle onto my back and took out a cigarette lighter. Each time I woke up as he struck the light. At the clinic they said that the burns hadn't properly healed and I should take another two weeks off. But I wanted to get back.

When I returned to the site I found that things were much the same. No one mentioned the accident. Ron probably thought I'd done something idiotic with the boiler. I didn't know how much Tamati had seen. Chug left me alone. There had been no rain now for months, and the fine red dust that covered the site billowed around my feet as I walked. The mountain pass above the site was lost in a bluish heat haze. I had grown to hate the endless burning sun and did everything I could to stay in the shade. The shaft had reached its maximum depth, and all that remained was to widen its lower half. Although I was grateful to be down the shaft and out of the heat, the drilling was even more difficult now that my right arm was bandaged. The arm was stiff and awkward, and I couldn't prevent the grit working its way under the dressings and infecting the burns. On my third day back the bandages began to give off a damp, sour smell, and that same afternoon I dropped the jackhammer down the shaft and smashed it. I had been drilling for half an hour and my arm had become painful and clumsy. As usual my eyes were squeezed shut against the spray of grit and water. A piece of rock came away from the wall and I lost my balance in the bucket. The handle of the jackhammer was jerked out of my grip. With my good hand I grabbed the rubber air hose, but the weight of the falling hammer tore it free. After a few seconds I heard the heavy tool crash into the bottom of the shaft. To my dulled hearing the noise seemed faint and distant. The shaft had been pumped dry, so there was nothing to cushion the impact. I looked up and saw three heads silhouetted against the circle of blue.

There was silence, then Chug called down, 'Naughty boy.' The words echoed up and down the gloomy shaft, fading and turning in on themselves. I stood very still in the bucket, rocking gently in space. I looked at the dark sweating rock where the slab had come away. I thought about my old job, night cleaning, and somehow it seemed attractive now. The bad hours and low pay were no longer important. Suddenly I felt a surge of relief. Although I knew Ron would be angry about the drill, I felt free of them all. When I had finished what I had to do I would try to get my old job back again. Soon I would be away from the sun and the dust and the noise, working alone in cool, quiet buildings in the middle of the night.

When the jackhammer was hauled out of the shaft I could see it was stuffed. A crack ran the length of the casing. Chug gave a low whistle between his teeth. Ron stood over it silently for a while, then said he was driving into town for a replacement. He told us to start digging rubble from the bottom of the shaft. Then he turned to me. He sounded annoyed.

'And you'd better come with me and get that arm seen to.' Yellow stains had begun to seep through the bandages. I shook my head, and felt suddenly dizzy. I had to concentrate to avoid stumbling.

'It's OK,' I said. I didn't want to miss this chance. When Ron was on the site he always kept one eye on what was happening at the tube. He shrugged and walked over to the Landrover.

46

'I'll be back in a couple of hours,' he called. A swirl of dust followed the Landrover up the track to the road. Chug wandered over to a pile of steel rods to smoke a cigarette before going down the shaft. Tamati climbed into the cab, picked up his book and waited for Chug. When Chug was out of sight behind the crane I went to the bucket. Its long handles were attached to the crane wire with a heavy U-bolt. A pin prevented the bolt from vibrating loose. I looked up at Tamati. He seemed to be deep in his book. With a pair of pliers I tapped out the pin. Tamati hadn't moved. I unscrewed the bolt until it was a quarter turn from being loose. I walked away from the bucket, glancing up again at the cab. Tamati was staring at me. His expression told me nothing. It was possible he'd seen me loosening the bolt. The dizziness returned and I put both hands on the rim of the tube to steady myself. I stayed like that for several minutes, my heart pounding, waiting for Tamati to speak. But he said nothing and eventually Chug appeared from behind the crane. He flicked the butt of his cigarette down the shaft. I watched the glowing point dart into the gloom. He picked up a shovel, climbed into the bucket and motioned to Tamati.

'Hoist away, hori,' he said, too softly for Tamati to hear, then looked at me and yawned. The wire went taut and the bucket rose off the ground. Tamati swung the crane around and Chug was lowered past me into the shaft. I gripped the hot metal rim of the tube and watched him go down. Once my eyes had adjusted to the darkness I could see him clearly. At about half-way the bucket jerked to a stop. A wave of sickness came over me and I stood up straight and looked at the cab. Tamati was adjusting the controls. The wire began to move again. When the bucket reached the bottom, Chug got out and began to fill it with rubble. I walked away from the tube, sat down on the river bank, put my head between my knees and listened to my pulse thumping loudly in my ears. The bolt was being held in by the weight of the bucket. Unless the bucket hit the side on the way up, the bolt would stay in place. I had seen that happen only once, the time Chug had cracked his head. I sat on the river bank for the half-hour it took Chug to fill the bucket. The sun beat down on my neck and back. My arm had begun to ache with a constant dull pain, and I felt feverish and confused. Chug's words repeated themselves in time to my pulse. They invaded my head, and the harder I tried to make my mind blank, the louder they became.

Eventually I heard Chug call to Tamati. I got up unsteadily and walked back to the top of the tube. As the wire began to move I could just make out Chug's blond hair. I watched as he rose towards the sunlight. Now that the bucket was full of rock he stood on its rim, holding onto the handles with one hand. He was whistling a tune from a TV commercial. I leant against the tube, paralysed by his escape. His head came level with the rim of the tube, and at that moment Tamati jerked the jib of the crane to one side. The bucket struck the tube with a hollow clang and the bolt spun past my shoulder. For a brief moment Chug's face wore the same slightly worried expression I had seen once before, his forehead creased in a frown. And then he was gone without a sound. We heard the bucket hit the side again on the way down. A few seconds later came the deep boom as it smashed into the bottom of the shaft. After the metallic echoes had died away there was a short silence, and then Chug began to scream; faintly at first and becoming louder. The sound was strangely high-pitched, like a young child crying. I was still gripping the steel rim, and suddenly I found my stomach heaving. Unable to move, I vomited again and again into the screams, drowning them out with the sound of my retching. I seemed to be there a long time, hanging over the rim, emptying the hot, stinking contents of my stomach into the deep shaft. Finally I sat down beside the tube, and lay back against the metal, my skin prickling with sweat. I watched Tamati climb out of the cab and walk slowly over to the tube. He stood very still, looking down. Chug's screams were faint again now, coming only occasionally and dying away into a whimper. After about twenty minutes they stopped altogether.

An hour later Ron came back. Tamati went over to the Landrover and spoke to him. Ron dropped the equipment he was carrying and ran down the slope to the tube. He asked us why

48

we hadn't gone down to get Chug out, his face white and shocked. Tamati pointed at me. The sweating had stopped, but a chill had spread through my body and I was shivering violently. It took a long time for Ron and Tamati to get Chug out; he was jammed in the bottom of the shaft. Ron eventually came up with him in the bent and twisted bucket. His head and one side of his body were crushed and his face was spattered with vomit. Because of his size Ron and Tamati had trouble getting him out of the bucket. By the time they had lifted him to the ground they were covered in blood. Ron spread out an old green tarpaulin next to the bucket, and they wrapped him up in it and laid him in the back of the Landrover. As the Landrover bumped slowly up the track to the road, Tamati climbed back onto the crane and lit a cigarette. My shivering had stopped and I got up and walked down the bank to the river. The late afternoon sun was glinting on the water, and a cool breeze occasionally ruffled the surface. I knelt in the shallows, took off my shirt and washed my face and hands. The shock of the water on my face refreshed me and cleared my head. I could feel my strength returning. I looked around at the thick wall of trees that hemmed the site and ran down to the river. Apart from the faint call of a bellbird somewhere deep in the forest, it was very quiet. I sat on the bank and watched the cloud of dust left by the Landrover rise slowly over the track, until it mingled with the blue haze of the mountain pass and was finally lost in the dusk.

ARCHAEOLOGY

WE LIVED THAT summer of the war in a house that looked
down over a dry valley to the low blue wall of the Tasman Sea.
Between the house and the sea was a riverbed in which the
stones gleamed like polished skulls in the sun, and beyond the
riverbed, a grove of apricot trees, and when in the late morning
the wind came down from the hills behind the house, the trees
would stir quietly as though touched by the ghosts of the gold-
diggers who a century before had left the valley. Apart from the
apricot trees there was little in the valley but tussock grass and
the occasional ruined shack with its iron roof adrift and moving
cautiously with the wind.

We lived there, he and I, with his mother, who in the
mornings sat among the skulls in the riverbed weeping, and in
the afternoons crept silently through the cool rooms of the house
in search of insects. The house had stood now for a very long
time, and along the side facing down the valley to the sea was a
wooden veranda from which the white paint peeled and flaked
with the sun and the wind. In the evenings we sat on the veranda
and watched the dusk settle into the Tasman, and imagined, a
thousand miles beyond, the red disc of the sun hanging low over
the Australian deserts. We talked on these evenings of the war,
of which we knew almost nothing, and discussed our theories
about how it might have begun, about whether the exchanges
had stopped, but we had no hard facts on which to base our
theories, there had been no travellers on the coast road for
months, and our small plastic radio had for some time now given
us no news.

During the day we worked on the ground beside the house,
extending the small garden to several times its previous size and
constructing an irrigation channel to bring water from a stream
in the nearby hills. The channel had enabled us to grow a

number of vegetables in the barren soil of the valley, and had been put together from the remains of a sluice run we had found in one of the gold workings in the hills. On the day of its completion we held a small ceremony, for which Chris's mother dressed in her best clothes and made a short, incomprehensible speech, but when the clear water of the stream started on its new course between the timbers of the channel she began to weep and we had to cancel the rest of our little ceremony and return to the house. She lived between two rooms at the back of the house, every few days moving her possessions from one to the other, so that one of the rooms was always quite empty, the floor-boards dusty and bare and the drapes removed from the windows. When I asked Chris about this he shrugged and grinned in his nervous way, Maybe she gets bored in one room, he said, unembarrassed by the madness of his mother. He was seventeen, older than I was, and little taller, we had been friends now for a long time, and when our fathers were taken by the navy because they were fishermen and the war seemed inevitable, I had come to stay with him on the coast. Each day we went to the beach and took shellfish from the pale yellow sand for the evening meal, varying our method of preparation from night to night to avoid tiring of our constant diet of food from the sea. Afterwards, on the veranda, we listened to the radio, aware of the need to conserve the batteries, but there was nothing to be heard except the uninterrupted buzz of static, as though the waveband was being jammed by unseen electrical storms beyond the horizon. I watched the sea at dusk, searching for the flicker of distant lightning, but nothing disturbed the dissolving line of sea and sky.

The lack of news did not appear to worry Chris, he was concerned more with day-to-day matters, such as the condition of the water channel and his plan to build a boat so that we might catch larger fish offshore. We sat on the veranda one evening and he spoke about the boat in his quiet, sure voice. He had found some sound planks and a few pit-props in a working up the valley, he said, and he would carve the props into ribs and fashion a clinker hull from the planks. When I sat and listened

51

to Chris talk in this way, I found it hard to believe that our time in the house was anything but a long holiday, and although I had not yet made the connection between the war and the behaviour of his mother, I felt sometimes that her strange ways were all that prevented this from becoming a permanent delusion. Earlier we had heard her moving with her insect jar through the distant rooms of the house, and now she appeared beside us on the veranda, holding the top down rigidly on the jar, as though afraid that its contents might escape. Two grey moths lay on their backs in the bottom. Chris looked at her solemnly, Are you sure they're dead, Mum? he said. His mother examined the fragile shapes through the glass, holding the jar up to the lamp overhead, then abruptly disappeared down the steps into the dark. We heard her making her way to the riverbed, where each night she buried her catch on the bank above the smooth white stones.

When I could no longer hear the sound of her steps I said, What will she do when there are no insects left to catch? and Chris grinned, Maybe we can persuade her to come to the beach with her jar and catch fish instead. His mother had lost interest in the ordinary things of life, she did not have it in her to help with finding food or with cooking, and when, on Sunday mornings, I took her down to the beach to wash, she resisted me strongly, not so much from fear of the sea, but rather because she held something against it. When eventually I got her to the beach, she stood stiffly in the shallows while I scrubbed her with sand, she said nothing, but it was plain that she hated the sea-water on her body. The ocean that month was a glassy green, there had been no storms and the debris along the beach had remained undisturbed now for as long as I could recall. When I sat with my line in the sand, I could close my eyes and conjure in my mind the exact pattern of debris along the tide-line, from the scattering of bone-white pumice to the position of the last desiccated twig. They were long, empty afternoons, with just the burning sky and the flat green sea, afternoons spent locked into a trance that would be broken only by the jerk of the line around my wrist—and then I was alert, touched by a startling invisible life, a life I could never believe existed until the nylon was taut and running, sending back its message of terror from the swarming bed of the sea.

And the sky to the west did not change, I watched it as I fished, neutrally and without expectation, and at the end of the day I took the fish back up to the house to fry on the iron stove in the kitchen, and we sat at the table and ate and joked with Chris's mother. Sometimes she smiled and we would pretend that she understood our jokes, but we knew that in reality she smiled because of some unimaginable event in the other distant world that she inhabited. She had begun to look thinner and more pale of late, so that we pressed food upon her, we gave her the largest portions of fish, but she would often leave her food unfinished and no amount of urging would persuade her to eat any more.

One afternoon Chris and I went up the valley to the gold workings to search out wood for the boat he was planning. A century before, the upper valley had been well populated with men looking for gold, and above the stream bed we came upon a collection of derelict huts and their complicated arrangement of wooden parapets and sluices. We worked on a sluice run until we could free its boards with ease, digging to loosen the framework from the earth. Then Chris stopped and stood up, he held in his hand a long tapered bone from which he shook the remaining traces of soil. What's this? Leaning forward, he pointed the bone at my chest, he was frowning heavily, You are condemned to take this boat we build, and sail in her to the west for all eternity, he said, and I said, Don't joke, what kind of animal is it anyway?

We scraped at the earth at the base of the frame and came upon other bones, they were laid out in a pattern that twisted in under the frame posts, and after a while Chris said, I think it's a man. Maybe the miners buried people alive under their buildings for luck, like the Melanesians. But the skeleton was too large to be human, the bones of the legs were exceptionally long, and as we uncovered more of it, we could see that the creature had a thin, curved neck like a swan, but much longer and more powerful. Then I said, It's a moa. We both stopped digging and sat back from the skeleton. We shouldn't move it, I said, and Chris said, But who is there to show it to? We sat and looked at the bones for a while, a little afraid, aware that the great bird had remained undisturbed for a thousand years. Then Chris said that we should collect the bones and take them to the house, where we could piece the skeleton together again, it would be safer there, though safer against what, he did not say. That evening we sat on the veranda and tried to remember what we knew about the great flightless birds that had ruled the country before man arrived from the north and hunted them into oblivion. We argued about their size and colouring, and finally agreed that they had been as high as twelve feet, with powerful, scaly legs and a plumage of deepest blue. Chris was certain that they were predators, able to catch their victims through their great speed across the ground, but I was sure that they did not kill, that they were stately birds who were able to live quietly among the rich grasslands of the time.

In the days that followed, we laid out the bones in a shed beside the house and began to fit them together. I had made a sketch of how they lay and Chris had glued a piece of paper to each bone and numbered it according to my drawing, the way we imagined scientists did. Because the skeleton had been twisted where it lay in the earth, our attempt to arrange it in its true shape was based partly on how we imagined the bird must once have looked. We worked on the moa late into the evenings, the two of us crouched in the shed under an oil lamp with the bones scattered around us, arranging, adjusting, fitting and matching the pieces we had taken from the earth, until we were light-headed with the effort of it, and still the great bird lay stubbornly misshapen on the floor, less clear now in its form than when we had uncovered it first at the head of the valley. We had been working on the bird now for more than a week, and we sat defeated in front of the skeleton, looking down at the bones, which showed ashen white in the dull light from the lamp. Are you sure you didn't make a mistake with the numbering? I said. Chris stared at me for a moment without speaking, then turned back to the bird, and I wished that I had said nothing. We went up to the house and switched on the radio. That evening the static seemed a little more subdued than usual, and as Chris carefully turned the dial, I thought I caught the fragment of a human voice. I grasped his arm, Turn it back. We found the spot almost immediately, and for the first time in many months a broadcast filtered out of the night, a voice that was infinitely fragile, as though exhausted by continual battle against the static that choked the waveband. We could catch only occasional words and could make no sense of them, until without warning a clear phrase emerged, '. . . windsheer across the equator . . . cloud projected south . . .' before the voice faded and was submerged once more in the relentless surf of static. Chris looked up and shrugged, Just a weather report, he said. We discussed the static and what might be causing it, but as on previous occasions we could think of no explanation that sounded at all convincing and eventually we lapsed into silence. Chris's mother sat bent forward beside us, the insect jar on the table next to her unfinished meal. Chris said, Aren't you hunting tonight, Mum? It pained him to see her like this, hunched forward as though paralysed, he preferred her to be occupied with her inexplicable rituals of capture and burial, he felt responsible for her when she was still. His mother made no response, she was watching the night outside in the particular intent way she did from time to time, and I knew that she would remain like this until after we had gone to bed.

Next day the weather changed, and for the first time since the beginning of summer a haloed sun shone through high cloud. At the beach, where I sat fishing in the sand, the colours were bleached from the land and a dull wind blew in off the sea. I sat all afternoon without a bite on the line, day-dreaming of a port in the north where the days, the weeks and the months had been marked out by the coming and going of a rusted trawler in which men shouted and joked, and where the catch was tumbled still living onto a quay that smelled of bilges and diesel. Towards evening the shoals had moved offshore and I wound in my line, as the onshore wind strengthened and whipped the tussock on

55

the dunes behind the beach. By the time I reached the house the wind was funnelling up the valley to lift dust from the hills beyond and slamming the door to the skeleton shed. Chris was in the kitchen preparing sea-eggs and had filled a huge bowl with their translucent pulp. I looked at the bowl and he laughed at my expression, Have you seen Mum? he said. I shook my head and turned away from the bowl of pulp to the window, You left the shed door open, I said. Chris started up from the table, That must have been her.

We went to the shed and pulled open the door against the wind, inside the skeleton lay inert in the dust, the great neck curved towards us, as though straining towards the light. We had kept the discovery of the creature from his mother, not knowing quite why, and now for an insane moment I thought, She's found it and pieced it together for us, and then I saw that the creature was the same as we'd left it the day before, misshapen and incomplete. Chris bent down to examine the skeleton, then looked around the shed. Some of it's gone, he said. One of the long bones that made up the legs of the bird had been removed, and although we searched the shed and went through the pile of bones that we had failed to fit into place, we could find nothing. Then distantly, from down the valley, came the sound of his mother's voice. At first we could not place it as we hurried towards the sea, and then we saw her, a slight figure standing beyond the apricot trees, the great leg bone of the moa clenched in her hand, screaming her incomprehensible accusations at the Tasman Sea as the wind blew in out of the chaotic dusk.

The wind blew steady and warm all night without a break, and in the morning it was still high when I went to check on the irrigation channel, which was vulnerable to wind where it crossed a gully as a raised bridge. Chris could remember nothing like it on the coast, it came now from the west at a constant speed, so dry that it wilted the crops and cracked the mud in the riverbed. The water in the irrigation channel had slowed to a trickle, as though the wind had sought out the stream that supplied it and dried it off at its source. Since her discovery of the skeleton, Chris's mother had taken refuge in her room, and she would not come out, even for meals. She lay on her side in a corner, her knees drawn up to her chin and her eyes fixed on a wall, oblivious to the food that we left for her on the floor beside her mattress. She held in her hand the moa bone, which she would not let go of, and she gripped it so tightly that I could see the sinews in her forearm stand out beneath the skin. We tried to get her to eat, but she would not hear us, instead she moved closer to the wall, holding the bone against her breasts, as though afraid we would take it from her. We worked silently on the skeleton now, for several days the steady wind threw up so much dust that work outside was impossible, we spent all our time in the shed with the bird, shuffling the remaining bones through an endless series of patterns that made no sense, we did not talk, somehow we could no longer think of very much that we wanted to say to each other.

And then the wind dropped and on the same day we had a visitor. She came along the coast track in the late afternoon, she was about our own age, and her hair was cropped very short on her head. We had seen no one in months, and we watched in surprise as she came up to the veranda and threw her bag on the steps. She looked dirty and tired. Do you have any water? she said. Later we sat together around the table and ate, and she told us that she had been travelling for five days up the coast, and in that time she had seen no one at all. She had come across a number of deserted houses, the occupants it seemed had gone inland to the mountains, though she did not know why. After telling us this she was silent, and we watched her eat the sweet potatoes and shellfish we had cooked. She ate awkwardly, her jaw moved at a slight angle to her head, as though her jaw-bone had once been broken. It was clear that she was very hungry so we did not ask her more questions, we let her eat undisturbed. When she had finished the meal she looked up and spoke: In the south they said that Australia was caught in the exchanges. There was a silence, I looked at Chris, then indicated the transistor radio. Could that be causing the static? She picked up the radio, listened to a burst of static, then placed it back on the table and shrugged. I dunno, she said, then, Where can I sleep? I put a mattress in the room next to Chris's mother and left the girl to her exhaustion. Chris and I sat up late that night arguing about our visitor and what she had told us. Chris was inclined not to take her news seriously, he said that she did not look very trustworthy, and that the word of a total stranger should be treated with caution. But what if she's right? I said. Chris got up tiredly from the table, You think too much, he said, and went in to bed. Next morning, before the others were up, I walked down to the beach to look at the horizon. The morning was still and quiet beneath a burnt-out sun, and to the west a haze covered the sea. Nothing showed in that western sky, it was as blank as it had been all summer, an empty gateway to the continent a thousand miles beyond, and after a time I went back up to the house for breakfast.

I found Chris in his mother's room, crouching by her mattress, a plate of cold toast beside him on the floor. He was speaking to her in a new, urgent voice. You've got to eat, Mum, you'll get ill if you don't. She did not even look at him, she remained with her face to the wall, the bone still gripped firmly in her fist. He tried again. We have a visitor, she's from the south. If you come and have some breakfast, you can meet her. His mother pulled her knees into her body and huddled closer to the wall. Chris got up and we went out into the kitchen where the girl was finishing her breakfast. She glanced up as we came in and continued eating, carefully cleaning the last scrap of food from the plate. Who was that? she said without interest. My mother. She's ill, said Chris. The girl looked suddenly uneasy. What's she got? There was a long pause, and then I said, She seems to have lost her appetite. The girl said she planned to continue up the coast that day, she did not want to speak of her eventual destination, and in the afternoon she went off up the coast path with a wave, and did not look back. Later we found our last cheese and a tin of honey missing, and Chris said, What did I tell you?

We worried about his mother now, it had been three days since she had eaten, she lay frail and thin on her mattress and her

58

eyes were dark holes in a white face. I put the insect jar beside her on the floor and sat with her that evening, a lamp by the open window to attract the night insects, hoping that this might help her to rediscover her old obsessions. When she slept, her breathing came in shallow gasps, as though she did not trust the air to enter her lungs when she was not awake. I dozed in a wooden chair beside her mattress, half listening to the ocean and dreaming of the creature that once walked its ancient shore. The bird was very clear now in my dreams, its curved beak and bulbous, searching eyes, and in those eyes was an intelligence that spoke to me out of the past, there was some knowledge there that I strained towards but could not grasp, and in the moment that I felt I might understand, a subtle shift in the rasping breath of the sleeper propelled me awake, my palms moist with sweat and my heart pounding in my chest.

The keel of the boat we were planning lay in the garden, but the enthusiasm I felt for the project was gone, and I only half believed now that the craft would ever be completed. We disagreed over the way in which the hull should be fixed to the ribs, we seemed now to be opposed on the smallest of issues. I told Chris that the method he proposed was dangerously fragile and the fixings might part in a heavy sea, but he insisted that as the originator of the plan to build the boat he had the final word in matters of design. I had not seen him like this before, the old diffidence was gone and had been replaced by a hardness that was quite new. The house, which had seemed so large when I arrived in the spring, now seemed small and cramped, we could no longer escape each other there, and I spent more time away on long walks in the hills and along the beach. We continued to leave food for his mother but mechanically now, without much hope, for she had lost all contact with the outside, and I knew that only some change within the sealed world of her madness would free her to eat. She would not even let us wash her and gradually the odour of her body crept through the house until it was so sharp that it took away the breath, like a thin strong hand at the throat.

Often on my walks I would find myself at a place I recognised as being miles from the valley, without being conscious of how I had arrived there. One afternoon I found myself above the sluice run where we had discovered the moa. I sat on the step of the shack and stared at the mound of earth still fresh beside the hole we had dug. It seemed an age since we had found the skeleton, but in reality it had been only a few weeks. And then I was on my feet. Of course, how stupid we had been. Some of the bones were still in the ground! I was in the trench, scrabbling with my hands at its sides and sifting through the loose earth in the bottom, each pebble a lost fragment of the bird, I was certain that a few more inches would reveal the vital bones we had missed. Eventually I sat back against the side of the trench and examined my hands. I had driven a wood splinter into my palm and my nails were torn and bleeding. There was nothing in the trench, not even the smallest shard of bone, and as I sat there beneath the sluice run I thought suddenly how foolish we had been to remove the creature from the dry earth of the gold-field where it had lain undisturbed for so long.

When I returned to the house Chris was standing at the door to his mother's room. He was half turned away from me and did not move when I came in. What is it? I said. He turned as if to speak, his face drained of colour, but in the end he said nothing. I went to the door and looked into the dim room. The insect jar lay shattered on the floor, and with one of the pieces his mother had carefully cut both her wrists. The blood had dried to a crust that spread out on the floor before her in a crisp red sheet, and although she sat upright in her chair and looked across the room at us with round, interested eyes, it was clear that she was quite dead. She was dressed in her best clothes, the ones she had last worn at the ceremony we held to open the irrigation channel, and as I stood there in my shock, I thought, At least she looks like someone's mother again now. Later that afternoon we combed her hair and pinned it back the way she had once worn it, then we cut her fingernails, which had become ragged and bitten. When we finished we took her down to the river bank and buried her beside the smooth white stones, she was very light and either of us could have carried her there alone. The moa bone was still clasped in her hand and I suggested that as a mark of respect for her last obsession we should bury it with her, but in the end we could not bear to do it, to sacrifice in this way such an important piece of the bird, and before we lowered her into the trench we had dug in the flinty soil, Chris gently prised her fingers loose from the bone.

Somehow our work on the moa now became something over which we had lost control. We were drawn each day to the shed as surely as we were drawn each day to the sea for our food, there was some larger imperative involved that we did not even try to talk about, but which was as real as our daily routines of survival. We did not seem to be any closer to a solution, but we knew now that there was no question of not finishing what we had begun. Sometimes, after hours of work, we would find that we had entered a cul-de-sac we had left some weeks before, we were repeating our mistakes, and it was at these times that our task seemed most hopeless. We blamed each other for these errors, though little was openly said. Each of us now saw the other as an obstacle to progress on the bird, and often we would work for hours without a word passing between us, locked into the bitter isolation that our work had brought us. Chris had developed a rash that began on his back and spread to his neck, his face and his arms, until his upper body was covered with raised weals. I said that we should eat separately in case it was contagious, and that I should work in the skeleton hut alone, but he maintained that the rash was caused by the dry wind, which blew in off the sea every few days.

I was dreaming every night now, harsh vivid dreams that were more real than the days themselves. I dreamt of a beach from which the ocean has withdrawn so that the seabed is exposed to the horizon, a naked plain of sand on which stranded creatures struggle for breath in shallow pools. And I dreamt of a harbour where a young girl with close-cropped hair sits beneath a yellow canary in a cage. She is absorbed in her task, which is to cut with a pair of scissors a perfect circle from the sheet of paper she holds in her hand, and as it is completed, the circle becomes a disc that glows first red, then whitens to an incandescent heat, until it burns itself into the retina of my dreaming eye.

Parts of the irrigation channel had begun to collapse and we could no longer find the energy to repair the damage. The early summer had become a distant time with no connection to the present, the projects we had planned seemed to be little more than futile exercises that had diverted us from the more important business we were now engaged in. Everything was sacrificed to the creature, to the hut where the dry scrape of bone on bone, the scuffle of some emerging pattern on the dirt floor and the magnified whisper of our own breathing were the sounds that marked out the boundaries of our waking hours. By now our stocks of food were running down, we had no more sugar or flour, and although Chris talked vaguely of an expedition down the coast to one of the abandoned houses the girl had seen, I knew we would never go. At the beach, the shoals seemed to have moved away from the land, and on some days I caught nothing at all. Then one morning I found that the tide had marooned a huge swarm of jellyfish on the beach and in the shallows, and for three days fishing became impossible. They were a type I had seen very occasionally in the nets of trawlers that had been fishing in the tropics, their bodies a pale mauve flecked with pink, and I wondered how they came to be many hundreds of miles south of their home waters. After a few days they began to rot, and the wind blew the stench up the valley so there was no escaping it, it hung there in the house as it had once before, and I woke up that night with the sweat cold on my body, certain that Chris's mother was back with us, that she lay with her bone and her rasping breath on the floor of the room next door.

For three days we survived on rice and a little dried fruit, and on the fourth day the stench from the beach was so great that I did not even bother to check whether fishing was possible. Instead I sat on the veranda and repaired my floats. Chris came up from the shed and watched me for a time. Then he said quietly, Are you going to the beach? We had not spoken that day, and I shook my head without looking up from my work. He watched me for a while longer, then went over to my fishing tackle and began loading it into its sack. What are you doing? He threw the sack over his shoulder and started towards the beach, down the slope to the riverbed, picking his way among the stones, an arm extended for balance. I got up and leant against the veranda rail, a point of hot metal seemed to press up against my ribs and my vision blurred a little so that I had difficulty in following him as he continued down the valley. Then I was down the steps and after him, slipping and scrabbling in the riverbed, I could hear myself shouting, but what I heard made no sense to me. By the time I reached the beach he was wading out through the shallows with the line in his hand, the jellyfish a grey carpet that folded in behind him. I ran into the sea and felt the creatures cling suddenly to my legs, they had been dead for days but now they came alive in opposition to me. I struggled towards Chris, he glancing back over his shoulder, then turning and wading on towards the outer edge of the bobbing carpet. The creatures disintegrated as I forced my way among them, I was up to my waist in a soup of jelly and tangled filaments, I was getting no closer to Chris, but my blind anger drove me on through the stench that rose choking around me and through the insects that hung in clouds over the grey sea. There was no escaping the insects, they bit my neck and arms and lodged in my ears and in my nostrils, I was inhaling them, spitting their bitter taste from my tongue and wiping them clear of my stinging eyes. And then suddenly I was free of the swirling bank of insects and wading into open water.

Chris stood motionless a few yards ahead of me, gazing out to sea, and as I made my way towards him he let go of the line he was carrying so that it spun away into the clear water, the skein of invisible nylon unravelling as it sank. We stood there very still, up to our waists in water, and looked at our new horizon, a horizon across which stretched a shimmering band of palest green. It lay in a continuous arc that appeared to touch the coast to the north and south, but this was an illusion brought on by the scale of the thing and by the curve of the horizon, and I knew that it must still be far out to sea. Despite its distance I could see that it had an internal life of its own, it was illuminated from within by a flickering that appeared to be due to electrical storms and which disturbed its surface like the movement of eels beneath the surface of a pond. The beauty of the thing took the breath away, we stood there hypnotised for a long time, watching its imperceptible progress across the face of the ocean, until eventually I touched Chris's arm and we made our way back to the beach.

At the shed the bird waited for us in the dim light, its bones laid out as we had left them in clumsy imitation of its lost form. We knelt there in the dust of the floor of the hut and began to work, we handled the creature with a new care, weighing each bone with a patience that had previously escaped us, testing our patterns against a fragile image of a living form that seemed somehow to have clarified in our minds. At first we had the impression of a small advance, but the further we pushed the advance the faster we found the puzzle giving way before us, pieces of the skeleton that had lain awkwardly together all summer were dovetailing smoothly; rib, joint and socket began now to match with ease, until the coupling of bone on bone acquired an effortless momentum of its own, and the outline of a new, vital pattern began to take shape in the dust. There was no stopping us now, we were the agents of a mechanism that moved with some older and deeper logic, and which now that it had been set in motion swept aside the trivial errors and false starts of the past months . . . We were laughing and shouting as we worked, the long summer which had seemed to disintegrate around us outside the dim confines of the shed, the abandonment of our crops and our plans to build the boat, the decline and final madness of Chris's mother and now the cloud that had appeared out to sea . . . all this was a distant irrelevance when set beside the intoxicating power of the process that we had become part of, the rebirth of the great creature that had once ruled the shores of our ancient ocean.

When we had finished, we sat very quiet and very still beside our completed work. The skeleton expressed a perfection of form that reached out of the past and silenced us with its beauty.

It was much more than the proud creature of my dreams reborn into the present, it was the vehicle for a form of knowledge that had previously been denied us, and which was linked to the dry wind that had sprung up outside and was rattling the windows of the distant house. Chris knelt beside the creature and gently stroked the great bone of the leg. I stood behind him, my hand on his shoulder, and felt the slow flex of muscle beneath his skin. We were very close again now, we belonged there together in the gloom with the creature, and I knew then that we would never leave the hut, we could not abandon the bird at such a time. I heard the wind rising in the apricot trees beyond the stream bed, but all sound had somehow become external to the hut, and even later, when the wind was howling up the floor of the valley from the sea and beginning to pry with steady insistence at the door to the shed, it did nothing to disturb the deep, clear silence inside.

ON MY FIRST day working for my new employer I drove his tractor into a swamp. It was Helen who saved the tractor from muddy interment and so spared me the wrath of her father and instant dismissal. I had been driving towards the low hills at the back of the farm, gazing across the Waikato farmland to the purple tumble of mountains, too dazed, perhaps, by the burning sun to be very much concerned with the ground beneath the tractor wheels. I ignored the change in the rhythm of the engine until it was too late, and when I looked down the front wheels of the tractor had disappeared up to their axles. I sat there for ten desperate minutes, watching the spinning wheels clog up with viscid mud, while the heavy machine settled further into the swamp. She came running across the grass towards me, and above the racing of the engine I heard her shout something. I took my foot off the accelerator.

'Stop, you idiot,' she yelled. Stumbling breathless up to the tractor, she said, 'Can't you see you're digging it in deeper?' Her dark hair was cut short at the neck, and there were beads of sweat on her forehead. 'Take it out of gear. I'll get some wood.' Although the ground was too soft for the tractor, it was firm enough to run on, and she loped off towards a splintered stump on the edge of the swamp. Returning with the wood, she forced it into the mud behind the back wheels, and began to scrape clean the clogged-up treads. She did it quickly and methodically, as though she had rescued farm hands from a hundred different swamps.

'You've done this before,' I said. She looked up at me and scowled.

'Can you imagine what my father will do to you if we can't get his beloved tractor out of this bog?' I mumbled something about beginner's luck. Then in a show of defiance I said,

'There's no way of telling that this is a swamp. It looks the same as any other paddock to me.' She walked off a little way from the tractor. I watched her bend to pluck at a clump of vegetation. She came back, held up some thin stalks and looked at me with her pale green eyes.

'What are these?' she said.

'Papyrus.'

'Close. Reeds. Reeds grow in swamps. And tractors sink in swamps.' She dropped the reeds in the mud and wiped her hands on her backside. 'OK,' she said. 'Reverse gear, low box. Keep the front wheels straight and accelerate slowly when I say so. There's solid ground about ten metres behind you.'

I did as she said, gingerly letting out the clutch. The wheels began to turn, and the wood groaned as it was forced deep into the swamp. 'Take it easy,' she shouted. I was sweating and my shirt clung to the small of my back. The tractor pumped a dense cloud of diesel fumes into the air and lurched against the mud like a great creature resisting the embrace of a primeval swamp. Suddenly the machine was free and rolling backwards towards the firm ground, and Helen was walking alongside, intently watching the back wheels. 'Don't stop,' she called. When I reached the edge of the swamp I switched off the tractor and leant my forehead against the hot bakelite of the steering wheel.

'Thank God for that,' I said. She seemed pleased by this display of masculine frailty.

'When was the last time you drove a tractor?' I made a helpless gesture.

'I've tried to keep my hand in, but the authorities have this stupid prejudice about them being used on the campus.' She smiled faintly and flicked a blob of mud off her arm.

'Where do you go—Waikato?' I nodded. She told me she had just finished her first year at Auckland, and for a time, without conviction, we swapped established views on the two universities. In the end we agreed that their most important characteristic was shared—likeable, eccentric lecturers whose whims and vagaries were beyond any reasonable prediction. She propped a brown leg up on the front axle of the tractor.

'How did you get this job?' She didn't bother to disguise the surprise in her voice.

'Your father's ad. I just applied.' She pursed her lips.

'Maybe you were the only one who did.'

'That wouldn't surprise me, considering the wage he's paying.'

'You didn't have to take it,' she said. I shrugged.

'Times are hard for the self-financing student.' There was a silence while she lit a cigarette, and I looked at the family's modern, hacienda-style homestead half a kilometre away across the fields.

'Your parents live in town, don't they?' I nodded. 'In that old weather-board place with the sycamore,' she continued. I felt my irritation creeping back.

'It keeps the rain out,' I said. She glanced up in surprise.

'Hell, I'd much prefer one of those rambling old places to . . . that.' She jerked a thumb at the distant homestead, and as she did so a volley of shots echoed across the paddocks. She stood up and looked towards the low hills at the back of the farm.

'Who was that?' I asked. She continued to look at the hills, but her expression was different now.

'My brother,' she said. 'Earning some easy money.' She threw her cigarette down and screwed it into the ground. 'Dad will be back from the stock sales soon.' She started to walk off. 'If you want to clean the tractor there's a hose in the milking shed.'

I watched her move away across the grass and thought of my first meeting with her father that morning. I had been finishing the third cup of sweet tea pressed on me by her mother, when he walked into the parquet-floored kitchen in his work boots. He was tall, with a sunburnt face and a sharply prominent adam's apple, and as he gripped my hand I caught a trace of subdued anger in his distant farmer's eyes. He said that he was employing me to rid his farm of weeds. Then in an oddly formal way, as though delivering a small lecture, he began to describe the habits of the plants that threatened his farm. He laid out a map of the farm on the kitchen table and showed me the areas most likely to be infested with each of the weeds. Ragwort, he informed me, was the principal threat to his livelihood. Now and then he would stop and pluck irritably at a fold of skin over his adam's apple, as though reprimanding himself for being insufficiently clear.

He took me outside to the implement shed, where the new tractor sat between neat rows of agricultural machinery. He showed me how to operate the spraying equipment and in his flat, serious voice informed me that the oily green herbicide was dangerous if inhaled. I should be careful to stay upwind of the area I was spraying, he said. I had not used a tractor in several years, in fact, and when the time came to drive the machine down the race, I moved off with a dislocating jerk and a short skid. I looked back to see my new employer gazing after me and plucking thoughtfully at his throat.

When Helen had disappeared I drove the tractor to the milking-shed and washed the last trace of incriminating mud from its underbelly. Then I set off on a more careful route for the hills at the back of the farm. Early cloud had disappeared, the day had begun to get very hot, and I could feel the sun burning my skin. Summer had been late, but in the hills the greens of spring were already thinning to a sun-bleached brown. I spent the afternoon spraying weeds in the hill paddocks. The thump of the hydraulic pump, the slow, inexorable progress of the tractor and the beating sun overhead induced a pleasant, almost hypnotic sense of routine.

Later, Helen's mother showed me my detached room on the lawn behind the house. The hacienda and its surrounds gave an impression of recently acquired wealth. Set in the lawn beyond my room was a swimming pool, and beyond that, an elaborate shrubbery. I was to share my room with a massive freezer, and when I was alone I lifted its lid and peered into its misty, thrumming heart. Inside lay gleaming cuts of every conceivable beast, an icy welter of shoulder, haunch and loin. An unvaried diet of red meat, I soon discovered, was essential to the health and well-being of the family.

We ate that first evening in front of the huge bay window

through which, by day, the family surveyed its property. Helen's younger sister, a voluble eight-year-old, in looks a smaller version of her sister, began the meal with an account of what sounded very much like sexual intercourse between two swamp birds. Helen was the only one to show any interest. Their father, who was making his way through a slab of steak with controlled aggression, began to frown as Jenny's story progressed. Eventually he told her to be quiet. There were more important things to be discussed than swamp birds. Then he announced that the main sludge-pump on the farm had broken down. There was silence for a time, and irritated that we were unable to grasp the implications of the news, he began to describe the effect on life in the milking-shed. Jenny screwed up her face and pushed away her plate.

'You always put me off my dinner,' she said emphatically. Her father ignored her and turned to me.

'Any trouble finding your way around?' I shook my head.

'No problems at all, really.' I glanced up from my plate. Helen was carefully dissecting a carrot.

'There's a swamp,' he continued, 'between the barn and the foot of the hills. Don't drive the Ford into it, will you.' The others smiled at the thought of such impossible folly, and in that moment I was aware of just how unpleasant things would have been if we hadn't managed to free the tractor. I felt a crazy surge of gratitude to Helen. Helen's mother leaned forward solicitously.

'Would you like some more steak?' My mouth stuffed with food, I could only shake my head and smile. 'I hear you're studying at Waikato,' she went on. I grunted helpfully. 'And what subjects are you taking?'

'I've just finished my first year of sociology,' I said. Her face was pleasant and blank.

'Sociology. And what's that exactly?'

'It's the—uh—study of society.'

'The study of society?' Suddenly the notion that anyone should attempt such a thing seemed absurd and implausible, and

I struggled to think of a way of making the whole idea sound more convincing.

Helen said, 'Think of it this way, Mum. Society is like a complicated machine,' she glanced impassively at her father, 'a sludge-pump if you like—with components that have to work properly if the whole thing is to keep going. Sociologists study the relationships between the parts, and tell us which parts aren't working.'

'You're so dumb, Mum,' said Jenny. Her father looked at her in warning.

'I don't need a sociologist to tell me which parts of our society aren't working,' he said. Helen continued eating, and without looking up from her plate, she said,

'Wharfies, blacks and bloody civil servants. Or has the list been extended recently?' Her father stared at her, and for a brief moment I thought that he was going to hit his daughter. Instead he cut into his steak with a new ferocity.

For obscure reasons I felt responsible for the silence that followed, and with that came a need to undermine the subject to which I had committed three years of my life. I addressed a stain in the middle of the table-cloth.

'A lot of sociology is just common sense. I suppose you could say it's a way of untangling and improving common-sense ideas about society.'

'Well,' said Helen's mother in a bright voice, getting up to clear the table. 'Now we all know.'

I looked around to see that I was the only diner with an empty plate, and suddenly felt a little foolish, as though I had been revealed in secret gluttony. Helen's father leaned back in his chair, lit an acrid pipe, and unfolded a newspaper. Jenny wrinkled her nose and sat on her hands, and I watched the massive bay window, where moths battered themselves against the glass.

Helen spoke to me with exaggerated politeness. 'There's ice-cream for dessert. Would you prefer vanilla, hokey-pokey, boysenberry or chocolate?' Her mother corrected her from the kitchen. Two of the flavours were off. 'You'll find that we eat a lot of ice-cream here,' Helen went on, without waiting for me to choose. 'I hope you like it.'

'I like it very much,' I said enthusiastically. Jenny's serious eyes regarded me from the other side of the table.

'Helen hates it,' she said. 'She says we ought to eat fruit for dessert. She says ice-cream clogs up your ovaries.' Helen leant over and gripped her sister's shoulder.

'Arteries.' Their father, who had been deep in his paper, looked up at Jenny's error. He was about to say something when the door opened and a youth about my own age walked into the dining room with a rifle.

Jenny jumped up and shouted something unintelligible about possums. Her brother ignored her and went out to the kitchen, where his mother began to make gentle, reproving noises about his lateness. He left the kitchen before she had finished, propped the rifle against the television and lowered himself into an armchair. When his father introduced us he stared at me for a moment, then jerked his head. Jenny asked, more clearly, about the possums. He held up three fingers.

'Two in a ditch and one in a blue gum.' He ran his hand through his hair. 'Took eight rounds to get that one.' I noticed then that his forearms and the front of his shirt were covered in a fine spray of blood.

Helen spoke coldly. 'What do you mean?'

'When they're hurt they dig their claws into the bark. You have to blast them loose. Sometimes you get half the possum and the rest stays clawed to the tree.' He spoke as though he found the phenomenon mildly interesting. There was a long silence.

Then Helen said, 'Of course. You'd only get half your bounty then, wouldn't you?' She looked at her father, pushed away her chair and got up.

'This isn't a farm. It's an abattoir.' She walked to the door and slammed it shut behind her. For a few moments our reflections in the bay window flexed and distorted. The rest of the meal proceeded in silence, and when it was over I retreated thankfully through the night to my outside room and its softly purring freezer.

For several days I saw little of Helen. Each morning I drove the tractor up to the hills at the back of the farm. To the east I could see the sweep of the Waikato plain, with its endless varieties of rectangular green, from the pristine sleekness of maize to the startling emerald of lucerne. In those hills the frustrations of a year of study were smoothed away. Layers of obscure detail that had crusted in my mind began to dissolve in the burning sun, and before the scale of the plain and the blue emptiness of the sky, my coming exam results seemed a puny irrelevance.

Further into the hills a line of bush—puriri, ponga and fern—formed a dense wall that marked the farthest point of the farm. Sometimes I drove the tractor up to the boundary fence, switched off the engine and listened to the stir of the bush, the vacant call of wood pigeon and the rustling of the hill winds in the tops of the pongas.

Steep gullies divided the hills and they had to be cleared on foot. I worked my way through the undergrowth with a long slasher. Encouraged by my isolation and the monotony of the work, I turned these occasions into heroic expeditions against an imaginary foe. I was alone in a parched landscape, stalking a predatory horde of plant life. The bright yellow heads of ragwort had developed terrible powers, and my task was to exterminate the plants before they carried out their malevolent plan to subvert the elected government of our small but significant nation. After tracking the ragwort along the gully bottom, I broke cover with a flank attack. Shouting dimly recalled comic-book war oaths, I flailed my way through the tangle of plants, scattering their stems in heaps around me, until I fell exhausted on an acrid carpet of flower heads.

I lay on my back after such an attack, staring at the cloudless sky, which had absorbed my shouts and the ragged train of echoes that followed. From the hillside to my left, someone called out, 'Now I've seen everything.'

Helen was walking down the side of the gully. She wore a faded red shirt and had one arm outstretched for balance. I jerked into a sitting position.

73

'What in Christ's name are you doing?' she said.

'What does it look like?' She stopped a few metres away and stared at me for moment, then burst into laughter.

'From up there it looked like nothing on earth. If you could've seen yourself, thrashing around like a madman and screaming all that Battle of Britain stuff . . . ' I had a sudden vision of the scene from above. I chopped at a desolate ragwort that had survived my attack.

'Wide open spaces have that effect on some people,' I said. She put her hands in the pockets of her shorts.

'You're not exactly first-rank farm-hand material, are you?'

'I'll just have to live with that.'

She smiled. 'The question is, can my father?' I pushed the slasher into the ground and leant on its handle.

'You'll be reporting on my progress then, will you?'

'Of course not,' she said. She paused. 'But why, for Christ's sake, did you choose this sort of job?'

I made a gesture that included the sky, the burning sun and the plain that stretched away to the mountains. She sat down on the side of the gully and began to look around her, as though a little reluctant to concede my right to the view. I pointed to the horizon.

'Over the Kaimais,' I said, 'if you look carefully, you can see gliders.' Above the range, climbing the thermal updraughts in immense, painstaking circles, were three delicate toys, sometimes disappearing against the backdrop of cobalt blue, and then signalling their reappearance at a higher altitude with a flash of sunlight from their slender wings. We sat on the side of the gully and watched them in silence. In the bottom of the gully the fallen ragwort began to curl and wilt in the heat.

After a while, I said, 'Your father is very serious about his scientific farming. The lecture I got on my first day could have been straight out of an agricultural textbook.' She pulled a face.

'It probably was,' she said. She leant back on her elbows. 'He didn't go to agricultural college, so to make up for it he tries to out-farm the experts. Nothing happens on this farm without a

74

chemical being involved. Then there's his grand plan to rid the farm of non-productive life-forms, as he calls them.'

I looked at the tangle of slain ragwort in the gully, and felt a twinge of remorse.

'That's what the hunt was all about the other night,' she went on. 'He pays my brother a bounty for everything he shoots.'

'I get the feeling your brother would be quite happy to do it for free.' She nodded and said nothing. The gliders had disappeared now and cloud was building over the distant range.

'Are daughters non-productive life-forms?' I said.

'More or less. He's a bit confused on that one. In his bones he feels I should be strictly ornamental, but his business instincts won't allow him to pass up cheap labour for the farm.' She pulled at some blades of grass and tossed them into the air. They were caught in the light breeze and carried down the gully towards the plain.

'He's that bad?'

She nodded. 'You'll find out soon enough.' She smiled. 'You're an ideal victim. You don't take your work seriously, and you're less than completely competent.' She pulled her legs up and sat tipped a little forward, her chin on her knee. Then she began to speak of her father. She spoke in the thankful but outraged way of someone about to escape an intractable oppressor, but who must leave others behind to suffer. She said that she only returned to the farm out of a protective impulse towards her mother and sister. She told me of her father's almost pathological fits of anger, of his incomprehension of his daughters and the relentless criticism of his son, and she spoke of her mother's naive benevolence in the face of it all.

'We've only been in El Paradiso, as I call it, for a year,' she said. 'The others got very excited when it was time to move out of the old place. The house was my father's reward for all those years of sweat. I think everyone half believed it would be a miracle cure for the family disease. But once the novelty of the architecture had worn off, we were the same vicious, warring bunch of people.'

She was silent for a while.

'So I've begun to hate the place,' she said, a hint of surprise in her voice. 'Sometimes I can't stand to be anywhere near it. That's why I'm up here.'

A long way off, somewhere on the plain, came the faint rise and fall of a chain-saw, a sound that somehow consolidated the silence in the gully, rather than broke it. I thought of the hacienda at the foot of the hills below us, and of Helen's mother alone in her elegant kitchen, preparing another meal of steak to be followed by ice-cream, yet one more in an interminable series that would continue year in and year out, until the last of her alienated children fled the home and she and her husband were left to grow into bitter old age together.

Abruptly Helen got to her feet. Her manner was cool and matter-of-fact again.

'You'd better get back to your ragwort,' she said, massaging a leg that had gone numb with crouching. She started to walk off down the gully, then turned back. 'Have you ever worked on hay?' I shook my head. 'They're mowing this week,' she said. 'Then you'll be picking up with my brother. Watch he doesn't drive you into the ground.' Then she was off, half walking, half running down the slope.

The meal turned out to be even more unpleasant than usual that night. Things began badly when for no apparent reason Jenny giggled during the short prayer that began the meal. Her father recited the same verse each night in a dull monotone, and on this occasion, through half-closed eyes, I watched Jenny's face pucker with the effort of containing her laughter. As the prayer came to an end she let out a high, uncontrolled titter, which was cut off almost immediately by a cuff to the side of her head from her father. We waited through an intense, hanging silence while Jenny sat stunned, her shoulders hunched in expectation of another blow. Then her father turned to me.

'You didn't use up much spray today,' he said.

'I spent most of my time chopping ragwort,' I replied. He grunted, and I noted with surprise that he'd gone to the trouble of measuring the level of herbicide in the drum. It was clear that any period of grace I might have had as a newcomer was over, and I would now be subject to the checks and controls endured by the rest of the family.

Helen had gone pale when Jenny was hit, and now she leaned towards me as though conducting an interrogation.

'Are you trying to tell my father that you can't spray and chop weeds at the same time?'

'It would be difficult,' I murmured. Helen's mother broke in with a question about the comfort of my room, and for a time she steered the conversation into inoffensive territory. Then Helen lit a cigarette, the first time I had seen her do so at dinner, and blew a stream of smoke across the middle of the table, re-establishing her presence at the centre of things. She spoke to her father.

'Speaking of that herbicide he's using, there was more about it in the paper today. It's been linked again to that stuff they sprayed on the Vietnamese. The stuff that deformed their kids.'

'Agent Orange,' I said. Helen nodded.

'That's it.' Her father's jaws worked on a piece of steak for a while.

'That spray,' he said, 'is the most effective herbicide on the market. I've been using it for ten years, and it hasn't done me any harm.' He waved his fork, inviting us to confirm his physical and mental well-being. No one at the table spoke, and the moths hurled themselves at the bay window.

Then Helen said, 'What sort of evidence would you need to convince you? A couple of deformed grandchildren?' Her mother got up quickly from the table. Her father laid his knife and fork on his plate.

'I'm not going to put up with this for much longer,' he said. Helen looked at him for a long moment without expression. Then she shrugged.

'What's one more lethal chemical anyway,' she said, with mock despondency. 'One of them's bound to get us in the end.'

After that, Helen withdrew from the conversation and her father and brother began to discuss the hay season that was due to begin the next day. It was agreed that I would occasionally help them out. At the end of the meal Helen disappeared and the

77

family settled down for an evening of torpor in front of the television. For some time I watched an awards ceremony, in which men in black suits and bow-ties presented each other with an endless series of bronze statuettes, all of which had been provided by a major manufacturer of underfelt.

Eventually I left for my room, where I lay awake nursing the sunburn I'd picked up in the hills. The close night made sleep impossible, and I lay sifting the events of the last few days and wondering absently whether Helen was preparing me as a sacrifice in the struggle against her father. Some time later there was a rap on my door and I got up to find Helen standing there. She held a large bottle of Black Label whiskey.

'My father's,' she said. 'It's too hot to sleep.' We found paper cups in the cupboard and chipped ice from the inside of the freezer. She sat on the freezer lid and I sat, in my dressing gown, on the end of the bed. She said that her father was unlikely to notice the loss. She topped up his imported whiskey with cheap South Island brands, a deception that she had been practising for a number of years and which he had never detected.

We talked of events at dinner, and she told me that Jenny had committed a similar act of profanity about a month earlier. At the time an unknown disease had been affecting her father's dairy herd, and he had hit Jenny so hard that she'd been knocked off her chair. She had caught her head on the table and required several stitches over the eye. Helen swilled her whiskey in the cup.

'What's frightening is his unpredictability,' she said. 'He'll be his usual dour self for weeks on end, and then some little thing will set him off. And you never know what it will be.' She gulped the whiskey. 'Occasionally you get a warning—when he does this.' She imitated her father's heavy frown and began to tug at an imaginary adam's apple. Some elusive similarity in their features made the parody hilariously true, and I fell back on the bed, choking on my drink.

Helen grinned. 'What he doesn't understand is that despite all the damage he does, he's actually pretty ridiculous,' she said. This observation, together with the sight of me coughing and watery-eyed over my whiskey, sent Helen into a train of giggles, and within a short time we were both doubled over our paper cups, hooting with slightly drunken laughter. Then Helen put her finger to her lips.

'My father's bedroom is on this side of the house.'

'He has his own bedroom?' She nodded, her face solemn. She said then that her mother had explained the move to separate rooms as a result of her father's snoring. But there was another explanation. On occasion she had noticed bruising on her mother's arms, and one morning had surprised her dressing and was startled to see a large bruise on the back of her thigh. Her mother passed it off as a fall on the steps.

The whiskey had leaked from Helen's paper cup. She placed the cup on the freezer top and watched the amber liquid collect in a pool around its base.

'You'd think he'd be content with beating the hell out of Jen from time to time,' she said soberly.

'How can you be sure? About your mother.'

'I can't. It's a guess.' Helen lifted her paper cup and finished the remaining whiskey in one gulp. 'I'm getting depressed again. Do you want a swim?'

'A what?'

'It's strictly forbidden to use the pool at night,' she said. 'Can you think of a better reason?' I finished my own whiskey, and felt a surge of careless exhilaration.

'Why not?' I said, and stood up a little unsteadily in my battered dressing gown. Outside the night was warm and the air carried the nocturnal odours of the farm: the musty scent of swamps and the deeper, sickly smell of silage stacks. We walked to the pool, which was sunk near fruit trees at the bottom of the garden. Helen took her clothes off and left them under a tree, her limbs flicking palely in the darkness. She crouched by the pool, shivering, then looked up.

'It'll be a bit clammy, swimming in your dressing gown,' she said in a whisper, then tipped forward into the water and was gone. I took off my dressing gown and tried to copy her silent, seal-like entry. The water had held the heat of the day and was

79

warm to the skin. I floated, waiting for Helen to reappear, the dense night pressing around me.

Light from the stars caught delicate patterns of motion on the surface of the water, crescent-shaped rills that spread out to the ends of the pool, then opposed themselves in fading arcs. Helen seemed to have been submerged for an impossible length of time, and I was beginning to feel a slight edge of panic, when I was struck so powerfully in the stomach that I doubled up and sank, swallowing water as I went down. When I came to the surface, choking for air, Helen was treading water close by.

'I only meant to surprise you,' she whispered, gripping my elbow. I made for the side of the pool, where I gripped the rail for a while, sucking in air. Helen hung on the rail beside me.

'Do you do that sort of thing often?' I said eventually. She leaned forward and placed a hard, chlorinated kiss on my mouth. Then we were clinging together, uncertain of ourselves, trying to stay afloat, dazed by the contact of our bodies. Helen caught my arm and we swam to the shallow part of the pool, where half submerged in the tepid water, I slipped inside her. For a moment we were very still. I looked towards the house, a dark rectangle at the top of the lawn. She bit my ear and laughed softly.

'My father isn't going to like this at all.'

'We could try to get it included in the contract,' I said, hoarsely. She pushed her tongue in my ear.

'If you make me laugh, your brother will come out and shoot us,' I said.

'No. He hates having to clean the pool.' She was moving against me now, and the water slapped lightly on our skin. And then we were lost to it, fucking only each other, oblivious to the house, the brother, the sleeping father. There was an urgency in her love-making, a desperation that seemed to have its source in the sour earth of the farm, to draw on the night air with its odours of must and decay, and yet somehow, in its strength and obstinacy, to counter the poison that her father had brought to the land.

Afterwards we lay in the shallow water and Helen talked of

80

the constellations overhead. Some of the more obscure of these had to be viewed from particular angles, she said, so I floated on my back while she turned me to and fro, speaking quietly of Centaurus and the Southern Cross.

In the following weeks, I walked and drove over the browning hills of the farm, chopping, slashing and spraying my way towards the elimination of all noxious plant life on the property. I was unsupervised and could take the work at my own pace, and if there was too large a quantity of spray left in the drum at the end of the day, I would tip out some of the liquid before returning to the house. Helen came up into the hills when her father would not notice her absence, and we made love in one of the upper gullies among the acrid ragwort, the January sun stinging our bodies. Then she would pull on her jeans, light a cigarette and tell me about her childhood. She told me of car journeys over the winding Kaimai passes, during which her father smoked his poisonous pipe. The children would have to vomit in their laps before he would open a window. After one such trip, she stole his pipes and threw them into a flooded quarry, and later, when none of the children would admit the theft, he beat all three to be certain of having punished the culprit.

'My brother's suffered more than any of us,' she said. 'Yet he's well on his way to becoming a carbon copy of his father. Like those prisoners in concentration camps who began to imitate their guards.'

Some afternoons I picked up hay with her brother, and on these occasions minimal conversation took place. I didn't know whether his attitude to me was part of a generalised sourness, or whether I was being singled out for special hostility. We worked together into the clear evenings after the baler had left the paddocks, one of us driving the hay truck, the other throwing the bales up onto its flat deck. It was a back-breaking task, with the driver controlling the rate at which the loader worked. When he was at the wheel, my partner made certain that I worked at the maximum possible speed, and I was careful to ensure that he did the same. As a result we were an efficient team, and Helen's father, who was now looking for evidence of my incompetence, had no reason to complain.

One evening Jenny came running into the kitchen shouting that two pukeko had wandered onto the back lawn. In a voice squeaky with indignation, she told us that her brother was about to shoot them. Helen and I went outside. Attracted by the water, the swamp birds moved along the edge of the swimming pool with their distinctive jerky walk, the deep blues and reds of their feathers intensified by the late afternoon light.

It was unusual to see the birds so far from their home in the swamps, and we stopped in surprise at the bottom of the steps. A movement caught my eye, and further down the lawn I saw Helen's brother kneeling in the shrubbery, his rifle trained on the pool. At that moment he fired, and the smaller of the birds stumbled on its spindly red legs and collapsed beside the pool. It beat its wings against the concrete until its convulsions tipped it over the edge into the water. The other pukeko stood quite still, immobilised by the death of its mate. Jenny had followed us onto the lawn, and began to wave her arms.

'Pukeko, run away,' she yelled in a shrill, angry voice. The bird remained motionless, and then Helen was running down the lawn. She jumped over the shrubbery, grabbed the rifle by the barrel and tried to wrench it from her brother. They struggled briefly, then Helen jerked the stock into his stomach so that he let go of the weapon and sat down, winded, on the grass. The surviving bird now strutted away in a zigzag path towards the fence.

We walked to the pool. The dead bird floated in the corner, a sodden clump of feathers, its colours dulled by the water. Helen smashed the sights of her brother's rifle against a fruit tree and walked over to where he sat beside the shrubbery. She dropped the rifle on the ground.

'Pukeko are tapu. If a Maori finds you shot one you'll be marked for life.' A muscle worked in his face and he looked up at her with open hatred. But I could see that he believed what she said. Later that night, when Helen came to my room, I asked her where she had learned that the birds were sacred.

'Nowhere,' she said, as she pulled off her clothes. 'But if they're not, they should be.'

Her brother had his rifle sights repaired and within a few days had resumed his killing. Often during the afternoons I heard shots echoing up into the gullies where I worked. On occasion it seemed to Helen and me that he was watching us, so we became more careful. When we met in the hills we first made sure that he was working on some distant part of the farm. On the warmest nights we went to the fields of maize at the front of the farm and made love among the high stems. Always there was the same impatience in Helen's love-making, a desperation that surprised me with its strength, that seemed to go beyond our fucking to the knot of hatreds at the heart of her family, and that convinced me that our time together meant something to her that I did not understand. Afterwards we lay in the warm earth and listened to the silence of the Waikato night, which was broken occasionally by a light breeze in the maize, or the ancient, reproachful call of a morepork.

By now it was clear that Helen's father was unhappy with my expertise as a farm hand. His checks had become more frequent, more unpredictable, and despite Helen's advice on how best to evade these checks, I found myself being caught out more often. I was responsible for maintenance of the tractor, a task to which I was especially ill-suited, and if the oil ran low or the injectors blocked, my employer would take care to point out my failure. One afternoon I was filling the spray drum without a funnel, and spilt a quantity of the expensive herbicide. He came into the implement shed as I was cleaning it up and watched me in silence, plucking at his throat.

'Do you know the price of that stuff?' Helen and I had been up half the night, and I was careless with exhaustion.

'Two hundred dollars a gallon,' I suggested.

'About half that. And if you spill any more I'll take it out of your wages.' He turned and left the shed.

At the dinner table that evening Helen's father said nothing at all through the first course, and he ate his steak with a deliberation that was unusual even for him. Then, as we waited for his dessert, he said to me,

'I've decided I won't need you after this week.' I looked at him in surprise. He had advertised for three months' work and I had only completed two.

'And my contract?' I said.

'There wasn't one.'

'There was an agreement for three months' work.' He took his pipe and tobacco from the window-sill and began to pack the bowl. He lit the pipe and frowned at me through a cloud of pale blue smoke.

'The agreement didn't include endangering expensive machinery. Today my son found tractor marks in the swamp. Why wasn't I told?' Helen gave a short, hollow laugh.

'Because you would have sacked him on the spot,' she said. Jenny turned on her brother.

'You fucking tell-tale,' she said. The venom in her voice was so incongruous in an eight-year-old that I almost laughed aloud. Her father reached out to strike her, but she got down from the table and moved out of his range. His hand shook as he gripped the bowl of his pipe and expelled another cloud of smoke.

'Anyway, there's less clearing than I thought. I can't afford to keep you on if there's no work for you.' I knew that he was lying, but he was clearly determined to be rid of me, and it seemed unlikely that anything I could say would change his mind. Helen was less easily persuaded.

'That's not true. There's another two months' work in those gullies,' she said.

'Are you calling me a liar?' he said angrily. She held his stare for a silence that seemed absurdly long, a silence that stretched out until it absorbed us all and which was broken only when her mother arrived from the kitchen with the plates for dessert. The second course took place in further silence, and at times the chink of spoons on china seemed impossibly loud. Helen's face was white and pinched at the nostrils, as though she had been holding her breath for an unbearably long time. At the end of the meal her mother was clearing the dishes, when her brother spoke in his flat, emotionless voice.

'I was cleaning the swimming pool this afternoon. Look what I found.' He took out an envelope and from it produced a small translucent bag, which he held up to the light. It was a used condom. Jenny got up on her chair.

'Let me see,' she said, and stretched out her hand to touch the dangling sac. Her brother jerked it away. He leaned across the table and held it in front of me.

'Here. It's yours, isn't it?' Helen and I had never used a condom, but mesmerised by the scrap of plastic with its milky-grey tip, I could say nothing, I was groping for an explanation, and sensing a conspiracy that I did not understand. Helen's father removed his pipe and thrust his sunburnt face forward in puzzlement.

'Is it yours?' he demanded. I began to shake my head. Then Helen got up, walked around the table and locked her arm, very tight, around my neck.

'Not his,' she said. 'Ours.' Her voice was calm, but I could feel her heart beneath her breast.

Her father's face was vacant with incredulity for a few seconds. Then he started to speak, from the throat, as though unable through shock to pronounce the words with lips.

'You bitch. You filthy little . . . ' In one movement he pushed back his chair, got to his feet and punched his daughter in the face.

Helen was knocked backwards against the table, and then she slipped off it, pulling the cloth with her, and sat down heavily on the floor. Without being conscious of having moved, I was in front of her father, a dessert spoon gripped in my fist, a futile impromptu weapon. Then her brother had my arm and was doubling it back behind me, and I felt the muscle in my shoulder tear. Her father took hold of my shirt at the neck and pulled me towards him. I was close to his face, staring into eyes glazed over with rage.

'Get out,' he said. 'Get off my farm.' Behind me I heard Helen trying to stand up, then falling down. I pulled away, and her brother released my arm. She was sitting with her head between her knees, spitting blood on the carpet. I knelt beside her and wiped the blood from her face with a corner of the table-cloth. Milk from the spilt jug had run off the table and matted her hair. She got slowly to her feet, pressing a bloody handkerchief against her face.

'Well that's it, isn't it?' she said quietly, her voice muffled by the cloth. The words fell into a profound silence around the table. Her father was frozen into a posture of aggression, his chin forward, his hands clenched at his sides. I saw her mother standing in the kitchen doorway, a dessert plate in each hand. On the table the condom lay forlornly in a puddle of milk, an obscene fish in a small white pond.

Helen's brother looked at us blankly, and I was certain then that he felt no particular emotion about what he had done—neither elation nor guilt. It was a simple, perhaps even automatic, act of revenge. Helen took the handkerchief from her face, then pressed it against her nose and mouth to see if the bleeding had stopped. She crumpled the bloody cloth into a ball, dropped it on the table and walked from the room. I followed her out. At the time I walked through the door, nobody in the room had moved.

In the morning we were up very early, and I stuffed my things and a few of Helen's clothes into my old holdall. We left the house in silence, making our way down the drive through the dawn. At the implement shed the tractor sat blue and massive in the gloom. I started the machine and Helen climbed up behind the seat. The sound of its engine, I thought, would be inaudible from the house. The road to the bus stop wound along the perimeter of the farm, and we watched the familiar paddocks pass without speaking. Over the hills a delicate pink light was flooding the sky and being absorbed by the feathered edges of high cirrus. The mutter of the tractor engine seemed hardly to touch the cool clear silence of the dawn. At the bus stop Helen got down from the tractor and I turned it back through a gate onto the farm. Half-way across the paddock I set the throttle, pointed the machine in the direction of the distant farmhouse and jumped down from the seat. The machine accelerated away across the farm, its double rear wheels throwing up a spray of dew from the grass.

Helen was sitting on the holdall at the bus stop and she looked up when I returned. She had a bruise, now yellowing, on her cheek and a crust of dried blood over a ragged cut on her lip. 'If it misses the house,' I said, 'it might try to find the swamp.' She smiled with difficulty and gripped my arm. We sat together on the holdall beside the deserted country road, watching the dawn light carve out then gradually illuminate the deep gullies in the hills behind the farmhouse.

Shortly before the bus came the hills began to echo with the first shots of the day.

CAST IN GLASS

TO BEGIN WITH I trusted the furnace. Like anything that's important in your life, you don't want to judge too quickly—you like to give the benefit of the doubt. So at the start I put my faith in the furnace; it had a quiet strength, whispering at me from the end of the long shed. From my first days on the lehr I knew I was part of a mystery—the creation of glass from raw sand—and the furnace was at the heart of it all. But there are two aspects of creation, and it's only now that I can see the other side. The evil side. For everything that is created, something is going to be destroyed.

You might say it's odd to think of the furnace as a creative force at all. Most people can't see the attraction in glass. But if you live with bottles every day, spinning them in your hands and looking into their depths, you begin to see the the beauty all right. It's not something you can put into words. Recently I asked G. Grinner whether he appreciated this aspect of the glass. G. gave me his grin, the most hopeless grin in existence, which could have meant anything, as it's just about the only answer he has. I thought about this for a week and then decided that G. Grinner saw the beauty too. You couldn't work for sixteen years on the lehr and keep grinning like that unless you saw into the heart of the glass.

G. has the most limited vocabulary of anyone I've known. The story goes that when he arrived on the lehr he could only sign a 'G' on his contract, he couldn't write his name. So the foreman chose his name for him, picking on his grin for identification. Ever since then he's been G. Grinner. Old G. really strikes you on first meeting. His eyes are pinkish and he doesn't have a lot of colour. His hair and lashes are pure white and his skin is almost transparent. He likes to keep out of the daylight, which is why he's been on the night shift for so long.

We work lehr number seven, and to be honest, G. could almost run the lehr himself. He's that fast. To see G. with eight Pepsis at once, spinning them like tops, is an education for anyone. You could never accuse G. of being talkative, and when I first told him that I saw the furnace as the creative centre of the factory, it was some time before he made any comment. Ten days to be exact. And then all he said was 'Don't tell Hankel,' and let loose that smile. I should say that Hankel is floor overseer and that he's the worst advertisement for mixed breeding you'll ever see. If you've been thinking of getting involved in mixed breeding then you ought to meet our floor overseer first. You might cancel your plans. Hankel is half-German and half-Samoan and he's got one of those moustaches that refuse to grow. It's shiny black, and you can see right through it to the skin. He hates the world for something, and it could be because of that moustache.

You couldn't say that number seven is one of the glamorous lehrs. We don't get many class bottles on our line. Old G. Grinner has worked on number seven since he arrived, and he's never been anywhere near the prestige lines. Hankel uses up most of his aggression on the unglamorous lehrs. He'll come up behind you and catch a discard on its way into the bin. If there's no flaw in that discard you can expect a certain amount of humiliation. It's surprising how much hatred there is in a man who is having problems with his facial hair.

So there's me when I first began, juggling these burning bottles like a maniac, trying to pick the flaws before I even knew what to look for. Opposite there's old G., four in each hand, spinning them like a machine made specially for the job. In those early weeks I was throwing out every tenth bottle for appearances. After Hankel had caught me a few times my future on the lehr began to look doubtful. I was getting near to desperation. Then old G. stepped in and showed me how to pick the flaw, to angle the bottle and look for the flash of silver. He also said to bathe my hands in meths each day to toughen up the skin.

Even with my hands roasting and Hankel cruising around like

89

some kind of shark, even then I was fascinated by the glass. At the start there was the furnace, two hundred metres away down the shed, sitting there making its dull whisper, feeding day and night on sand and oxygen. It was at the centre of the factory that furnace, everything followed on—the operators, moulders, sorters, packers, drivers. I once tried to add up how many men worked for the furnace and I lost count at three hundred. They wouldn't let you anywhere near the furnace—the bosses that is—you couldn't get close to it without someone asking you what you were up to. Without protection the sound from the furnace was too much to bear. But once you had your plugs in all you could hear was this whisper, like the sound of waves on a distant beach.

After a while, G. and I started to work as a team. I'm not claiming that I got as fast as him, you can't catch up sixteen years overnight. But my hands had started to harden, and I'd learnt to handle the tricky bottles, like the square Jim Beams. They would vary the speed of the line, they could put you under a lot of pressure. By now G. and I were able to handle most of what they threw at us. After I'd been there about five months, G. and I became the longest-serving crew on the night shift. Even on the prestige lines they didn't stay long. The others got on to the day shift as soon as they could, they wanted to see their families. But the nights suited old G. and me quite well, G. because he couldn't stand the sunlight, and me because I'm not keen on crowds. I like to avoid gatherings of people if I can.

I took a professional interest in glass. I found an article concerning the glass-makers of Venice, which I took to work and showed to G. The best glass in the world is made on this particular island in Venice, and the glass-blowers there can produce any shape at all—fancy bottles, goblets, even small animals. Although G. didn't comment as such, he was quite interested in the place. One day when I had a bit of cash—let's face it, a lot of cash—I might travel to Venice and take a look at these glass-works. I could see myself being welcomed as a glass-worker from the other side of the world, and being given a guided tour of the place. I would hold up one or two of their items to the light, so as to illustrate the methods we used on number seven back home.

In the middle of the shift, when the annealing has been set up and there aren't many discards coming through, you get a bit of time to think. It's during those hours that I wonder about the furnace, or try to imagine what's going on inside old G.'s head. Hankel is asleep in his office and you can work with half your mind on the job. It was that sort of time (about five in the morning) when I nearly let through the bottle in a million. If you're sorting you're looking for the same thing all the time, the same old tell-tale flash. You're not looking for anything exotic. And that's the only word to describe this particular bottle. It was an ordinary Pepsi except for one thing. There was an insect, a small mosquito, in the glass of its neck. The thing about this particular insect was that he was in perfect condition. Something buried alive in molten glass—from head to foot, that is—shouldn't look too normal when the glass has cooled. But this mosquito was in perfect shape, and he just sat there in the glass, looking out at me. Me staring in and him staring out.

I called him Bill immediately. The name just came to me. I took the bottle home and placed it in the centre of my mantelpiece next to the article on the glass-makers of Venice. I studied that insect a lot, and spent some time thinking about how he could have finished up like that, locked into the glass. After a while I realised he was a gift from the furnace, and it wouldn't do to ask too many questions.

About this time we had some problems with the lehr. They'd started a new line, some cordial bottle that we'd never seen before, a really lousy item. The annealing wasn't right, or maybe it was just the design. Either way, we were throwing out three-quarters of the bottles coming down the lehr, hour after hour. There's a certain amount of satisfaction in doing this to a low prestige item. Sometimes they just didn't bother to design those bottles. Although they had their problems on the glamorous lehrs, Hankel always seemed to get more annoyed when things went wrong down our way. Now he was spending all his time cruising around us, getting upset about these unimpressive cordial bottles.

Hankel always wears the same headgear and I've never seen him without it. It's one of those floppy cricket hats with the wide brims. Once it was white, but now it's the colour of sump oil. When he's checking a line he pulls that hat over his eyes because of the glare from the glass. All you can see is this filthy hat, and sticking out from underneath, his unsuccessful moustache. Even with Hankel upset and cruising around the lehr, G. can't stop his grinning. It's something in his make-up. When Hankel is in that state I'm careful to keep a very straight face, but G. isn't under that sort of control. So there's Hankel standing next to me on the line with his greasy hat pulled down, picking up bottles for inspection. Opposite is G., grinning away under his invisible eyebrows, and tossing out three-quarters of Hankel's precious cordial bottles. Because G.'s got the fastest hands in the factory, there's nothing much Hankel can do to him. He's like a rare species that can't be hunted. But all that anger in Hankel has to go somewhere, so to make himself feel better he gets me to empty the discard bins. Emptying those bins by hand is one of the less desirable ways of spending time in a glass factory; it's usually done by fork-lift. There's not much more you can say about that particular job. Old G. missed his tea breaks that shift. It was his way of apologising to me for the problems caused by that grin of his.

It's hard to imagine a more ugly object than one of those partly formed cordial bottles. I took one home and positioned it on the mantelpiece to give Bill an idea of the sort of item we were sometimes asked to put up with.

On the big lehrs they were supposed to have a full crew of six, but it was unusual to see more than four men on the night shift. I suspected that those missing sorters had discovered some of the more unpleasant aspects of Hankel. He's the kind of overseer who can take the glamour out of any job. One night our cordial bottles got so bad that for two hours we took them straight off the line and threw them in the bins. Old Hankel was asleep in his office, he'd given up for the evening. My mind had been wandering a bit; I'd been considering my trip to Venice and wondering whether Bill might like to come along. I hadn't noticed anything different about old G. Grinner that shift; he'd been grinning away as he cleared those useless items off the line. Then old G. stopped smiling, looked at me in a strange kind of way, and toppled over on the line. I watched the bottles pile up against his body. I thought he was pulling some sort of joke. When he didn't move and the bottles started to smash on the concrete I went round and dragged him off and laid him on the floor. Someone from the next lehr went and woke up Hankel, and even though he could see old G. amongst the broken glass, you could tell that he wasn't too pleased at having his sleep disturbed. Old G.'s face had taken on a kind of bluish colour, and one of his legs was quivering as though it had a life of its own. Even when two men picked him up and carried him to the office that leg kept on jerking away. Later the ambulance came and they covered him in a red blanket and took him away.

As Hankel and I didn't communicate with each other as such, the next day I went down to Personnel. At first the girl wouldn't tell me anything because I wasn't G.'s next of kin. I explained to her that G. Grinner didn't have any next of kin. Then she told me that he'd suffered some kind of seizure and he was in intensive care. I stood there for quite a while just thinking about old G. I kept seeing those bottles piling up against his body like driftwood on a beach.

I was the only sorter on lehr number seven now and although they slowed the line, I was under a lot of pressure. They gave up on the cordial bottles and went back to the standard items, which made things worse. There's one thing that could be said for those cordial bottles—you could dispose of them fairly quickly. You didn't need to do any high-grade sorting to see what was wrong with them. So it was just me and number seven, my hands going like crazy, trying to keep up with that river of glass on the lehr. And in the distance the furnace, feeding on its sand and air and channelling the glass into the moulds and on down the lines. With old G. Grinner gone from the lehr there was nothing between me and the force at the centre of the factory. There were times now when that whisper sounded to me like some kind of threat.

I went to Personnel again at the end of the week to check on old G.'s condition. The same girl was there, though she'd forgotten who I was, and I had to explain it all again. She spent some time looking through her filing cabinets for old G. Grinner's records. It turned out that his file was in the discontinued section. Apparently G. Grinner had passed away the day after he went into intensive care.

I went home and broke the news to Bill. I explained the way old G. had helped me out at the start. I told him how G. would make up for the trouble caused by that grin of his. I described his eyebrows and explained how they were virtually invisible at times. To be truthful, I got quite emotional at this point. Bill was sympathetic, he sensed how close we'd been. I ended up telling Bill about my experiences on number seven from the very beginning. I spoke about Hankel's problems with his facial hair, about his cricket hat and about the time he spent asleep each night in his office. I told him about the beauty I saw in the glass and explained how the powers of the furnace were often squandered on items like those cordial bottles. A lot of the things I said had been damming up for a long time. Afterwards I felt a lot better. I hadn't forgotten about G. Grinner. Far from it. But I felt that I could go back to the lehr now and try to live up to old G. Grinner's standards of glass-sorting.

Bill and I cemented our friendship that night. Now I would go home and explain to him about the difficulties of running a lehr on your own and he would listen carefully if I was trying to get something off my chest. In fact he was the best listener I'd ever met. I began to consider the subject of death from time to time. It wasn't something I'd given a lot of thought to before. It seemed to me that if you could be struck down like that, it wasn't wise to delay those big plans for too long.

I was thinking of my Venice trip. I discussed the matter with Bill and we agreed it would be wise to start saving straight away. Without me asking outright, it became understood that Bill would accompany me on the trip. We did some calculations and I found that it would take me three years to save enough for that trip. You couldn't say they overpaid you at that factory. As it happened, a few days later old Hankel approached me at the end of a shift and asked me whether I wanted to work a double. That's two shifts in a row. He was almost polite. I thought about the Venice trip, and in the end I agreed, because I knew they had to pay you overtime for that second shift.

It wasn't too long before I lost track of day and night. That's what comes of working doubles. At the end of the shift I went home and straight to bed. Sometimes I didn't have a chance to speak with Bill, but he said he understood the sacrifices that were necessary. I often wished that I had introduced Bill to old G. Grinner, because I know they would have taken to each other. They had a lot in common. One night I apologised to Bill about this and he said that he was sorry too. It was one of those things, he said, and he knew I hadn't deliberately kept them apart.

About this time I began to notice a definite gap on the other side of that line, a G. Grinner-sized gap in space. That gap would get quite active at times, standing there under the fluorescents, sorting bottles without making any difference to the number of items on the line. Sometimes, in the middle of the shift, that gap would topple over amongst the bottles. When this happened I thought about the Venice trip, or some other subject, so as to take my mind off its antics. I was grateful it didn't have any features as such. I was just thankful it wasn't standing there grinning at me.

It's hard to say when I noticed the glass heating up. To begin with I didn't want to see the truth. I had a lot on my mind, what with responsibility for number seven lehr and trying to ignore the antics of that gap. Eventually I had to face the facts of it. The bottles were getting hotter every shift and the way things were going, soon I wouldn't be able to touch them at all. I gave the matter quite a lot of thought. I discussed it with Bill. We agreed there wasn't much to be done until we knew how hot the glass was going to get. I soaked my hands in meths like the old days, but it didn't make a lot of difference. I was throwing those bottles back onto the line as fast as I could, and spitting on my hands like a madman to try to cool them down. I watched the other sorters, but the larger lehrs didn't seem to be affected. I listened to the furnace for clues, but that whisper was in an unknown language—it could have been the language of another planet for all it meant to me.

And then without any warning the temperature of those bottles started to go down again. It continued all shift and on to the next one as a well. I sat in the toilets and thought it through. And then things began to fall into place. A pattern began to emerge. Arranged against me were forces beyond my command. Forces that could vary the temperature of the lehr at will. Forces that were able to set a small animal in glass without harming it in any way. Everything pointed to the furnace. I thought back over the previous months, and wondered how many of the small, unexplained events were its secret work. The whole of my time on lehr number seven was thrown into new light.

I couldn't discuss my discovery with Bill. As an offspring of the furnace himself, he could no longer be relied on. Wasn't it likely that he knew more about the furnace than he had let on? When I returned at the end of a shift the conversation between us was strained. He began to avoid my eye. I couldn't think of a way to raise the subject with him. At the factory I listened for signals from the furnace, for evidence of its next move. I was straining at the whisper now, I knew it held the key.

My respect for glass was gone. The beauty I once saw in the bottles now seemed an illusion. It no longer mattered whether I was sorting a prestige item or one of those cordial bottles. They were all the creations of the furnace, and the furnace had begun to show its true nature.

I felt alone now, there was no one to trust. The gap still made an appearance on the other side of the line from time to time, but you couldn't call that company. I was walking around in a kind of trance. I worked on the line in that state. I ate my meals in that state. I even slept in that state. I sat at the kitchen table and watched Bill on the mantelpiece, silent inside his bottle. We had stopped speaking altogether. I stared at him for hours one evening, trying to pressure him into an explanation. But he remained silent, and after a while I sensed it was me who was trapped in the glass and it was Bill who was out there staring in. I had to jump up and walk around to prove I wasn't stuck in that bottle. The feeling of being cast in glass came over me quite often after that. The only time I was safe was when I was moving about. I got to the point where I had to avoid staying still for any length of time.

My strength was slipping away. I didn't have the stamina for the struggle. I was falling asleep on the line. I'd never believed that it was possible to fall asleep standing up until it started happening to me. Then one night I realised something that should have been obvious all along. The gap on the other side of the line had been very active that night, sorting away at breakneck speed, then stopping and lying down on the line every ten minutes or so. While I was watching that gap perform it came to me suddenly that it was the furnace that had destroyed G. Grinner. I thought about this for the rest of the shift. I thought about the long years of service old G. Grinner had given to glass, and the way he had ended up on the concrete amongst those broken bottles. And I thought about his own respect for the furnace and about how in the end the furnace had turned on him. I realised that having destroyed G. Grinner the furnace had now set out to destroy me.

I was shaking as I clocked out at the end of the shift. I was still shaking when I walked into the kitchen. At first I couldn't talk to Bill. I paced around for a time. When at last I spoke, I began quietly, talking of the early days of our friendship, of inviting him into my home. I talked of my hopes for the Venice trip, of the two of us together in the world centre of glass. I took down the article over the mantelpiece and tore it up, page by page. I threw the pieces into the fireplace. I wanted Bill to suffer. I wanted him to feel some guilt. I talked about the doubles I'd worked, sixteen hours at a stretch to save for the trip. I talked of the gap, of its habit of lying down on the line. I asked him how anyone could be expected to put up with that for months on end.

I demanded to know about his relationship with the furnace. I was shouting now, I had lost control. But he said nothing. He just stared down at me from the mantelpiece and I felt again that it was me who was trapped on the inside, and he was out there looking in. I must have blacked out, because a moment later I found myself on my knees. I got hold of the mantelpiece and struggled to my feet. I grabbed the bottle and smashed it with all my strength against the hearth.

There wasn't much left of the bottle after that. The pieces scattered all over the kitchen. You might think I felt satisfied. You might think that I was wild with happiness. But it wasn't like that. I looked around the kitchen and in a corner by the fridge I saw the piece of the bottle that had been Bill's home. I knelt down beside that fragment of glass and there was Bill, looking up at me in this sorrowful kind of way. After what I had done to him he was actually gazing up at me with this look of sadness in his eyes. It was the sort of look that crushes you inside. Then I saw that Bill had been sent out into the world for a purpose. A kind of mission. I saw clearly then that he was the offspring of the furnace and had been issued forth into the world as its only begotten son. I had been so tied up with my own plans, with my trip to Venice, that I had missed what had been staring me in the face all this time. I picked up the fragment of glass and laid it on a dish. That dish had been left to me; it was the best piece of glass in the house. I put a cloth over the dish, to cover Bill's nakedness, and laid him out on the kitchen table.

I kept watch over Bill now. I sat beside him there on his crystal dish under the kitchen window and thought of his mission, and how I had nearly brought it to an end. I thought about his journey from the heart of the furnace, down the lehr and out into the world, and how I had been chosen to pick him from the line and give him shelter. I knew that to complete his work he would have to be made whole again. I bought some candles and placed them round the dish. I kept them burning through the night. You could say he was lying in state. I got quite emotional at times, seeing him there in his nakedness, exposed to the world. I felt closer to him now than ever, and although I knew he had to leave, it would be very hard when he was gone.

Before the shift I put out the candles and stood at the end of the table. Then I recited the chant I had made up for the occasion.

For you are Bill and I am me
Our time is up, it has to be

You came to me within the glass
And hid behind your sacred mask

We planned a trip across the sea
To admire the glass of Italy

How sad I am we'll never go
Our methods here, they'll never know

Your home is where the furnace roars
I'll take you to its open doors

I didn't understand your fate
But you'll be my eternal mate

Then I wrapped him in a table-cloth, put him in my lunchbox and left for the factory. I hid him in my locker until late in the shift, when Hankel was likely to be asleep in his office. I unwrapped him carefully, I knew the noise of the factory would be a shock after his months on my mantelpiece. He took it well. Even when I brought him into the main shed he didn't flinch. Hankel was nowhere to be seen. I walked up the line towards the moulding section, holding the dish before me. I had never been this near to the furnace, and even a hundred metres away I could feel the heat on my face. You only realised its size when you got this close. I was off limits now, but there was no one about, not even the furnacemen. The whisper increased until it seemed to pierce my head. I was happy now. I was on top again. For a long time on the lehr I had been struggling to understand. But now it had all been made clear to me. I had come to know the furnace and the mission taken on by Bill, its only begotten son. I had been chosen to shelter him in my own home, and now I was returning Bill to the furnace to be made whole. I was singing as I approached the furnace—it was the chant I had composed for the occasion. The chant was mixing with the sound of the flames inside my head, until they were part of the same thing. It was like one hymn. I was bathed in heat as I passed the reflector screens and walked towards the mouth of the furnace. I held Bill high on his dish. He was going to his home. The skin on my lips was cracking with the heat. I saw a furnaceman, his hand raised and his mouth open in a shout that was drowned by the hymn in my head. He was too far away to interfere. I stepped under the wire, and with the dish held out in offering, I went on towards the great clean heat.

HISTORY FOR BERLINERS

THE FIRST TIME I saw Jan and Klaus they were standing naked together in a dormitory in Lipari. Jan faced the window, his arms stretched out to the sill, while Klaus rubbed scented oil into his back. They spoke to each other in rapid German, their conversation punctuated from time to time by Jan's high laughter, and seemed oblivious to the conventions of discretion and reserve that tend to be observed by strangers in hostel dormitories. It only occurred to me much later that this little scene was for the benefit of the other Germans in the dormitory, physics and geology students who had come to the islands in order to climb the volcanoes and who never appeared in anything less than their sturdy mountaineering underwear.

The previous day I had taken the ferry from Sicily with these students, straightforward, friendly men with beards and professional-looking rucksacks. There had been a slow swell on the sea and the day had been very clear, so clear that we could make out a smudge of black smoke on the horizon in the direction of the discontented Etna. At the time the papers were reporting a scheme to redirect the lava flow of the volcano through a series of controlled explosions. The students were discussing the plan, in English for my benefit, and when they had agreed that it was an ingenious notion, one of the Germans turned to me and said, 'But of course we are in Sicily. First the old men of Palermo must be certain they can make money from this plan.' It seemed appropriate, somehow, that here in their ancient homeland the influence of the Mafia extended even to the regulation of volcanic activity.

In the lee now of the island's ashy shore, we moved across a mirror sea. Behind me the Germans were gathering up their rucksacks and securing their geologists' hammers to thick leather belts. The climax of their expedition, they had told me,

101

was to be an ascent of an active volcano on the outermost island of the group. They had brought with them an impressive amount of gear, and later, when I made my way up to the hostel through the narrow streets of the old port, the students preceded me like a train of Sherpas. I found myself feeling absurdly underequipped, as though by coming to the islands in order merely to lounge about and lie on the beach I was betraying the more serious geological obligations of the visitor to these parts.

In the morning the students rose early and either tramped into the interior of the island or caught ferries to the other islands in the group. After they had gone, I made my way down to the old port and sat with a cappuccino and a three-day-old English newspaper in a café. In order to avoid reading the newspaper, I watched an old man on the breakwater performing a mysterious operation with wine casks. Water was drained from the cask, fresh sea-water funnelled in, and a series of pebbles dropped through its bung hole. Each cask was then turned a little on its axis and wedged still against its neighbour. I had been watching this operation for half an hour, trying to decide whether it was a scientific procedure or an ancient superstitious practice, when a ferry drew in to the breakwater and unloaded its cargo of passengers. All of them, it appeared, were islanders returning from the mainland and they quickly dispersed along the waterfront, until the breakwater was empty again except for the old man and his wine casks.

At this point the two Germans from the dormitory emerged from a side street and ran down to the breakwater. When they saw the ferry, moored and empty, they stopped, looked up and down the waterfront, and hurried over to the old man filling his casks. It was plain from the old man's passivity and by the increasingly urgent gestures of the Germans that he was failing to provide them with the information they needed. Then one of the pair, the more serious-looking of the two, came across to the café to where I sat.

'Excuse me,' he said. 'We are looking for our friend. Her hair is cut like this,' he made a flat gesture across the crown of his head, 'And her eyes are not working.'

'You mean she's blind?'

'Sometimes she is blind, ja.' I thought of the steep drop from the breakwater into the harbour, but thought better of suggesting they look in the water. He continued, 'You were here when the ferry arrived?'

'I'm sure she wasn't on the ferry. I would have noticed her.' He called in relief to his friend, who was still trying to communicate with the old man. I noticed that his friend didn't break off the encounter straight away, as though reluctant to abandon the interrogation before the old man had shown some willingness to help. When he came across to the café I was struck immediately by how absurdly good-looking he was. Dishevelled blond hair, fine high cheek-bones and the shadow of a pencil moustache—the whole effect of ambiguous Prussian beauty was underlined by a mole on his right cheek in precisely the place where an eighteenth-century lady would have worn her beauty spot.

The three of us discussed ferry times for a while, and agreed that their friend was likely to arrive on the afternoon sailing. Then Jan, the blond-haired one, said, 'Your accent . . . you're not English?'

'I'm a New Zealander.'

'So. Sir Edgar Hillary. Why then aren't you with our Bavarian friends on the side of one of the volcanoes?'

'Sometimes New Zealanders get tired of climbing mountains.' Jan laughed the high, tense laugh I had heard the night before in the dormitory; not so much, I felt, at my reply, but because of the opportunity to continue the mocking tone of the conversation.

'Perhaps you will not be too prejudiced against us,' he said. 'We are from East Berlin.' I looked at his friend, who gazed back at me as seriously as before.

'You've been very enterprising in getting to Sicily,' I said.

'So. You're suspicious because everyone knows we Communists are kept locked up behind our borders. However, the father of Klaus,' he laid his hand on his friend's shoulder as though introducing an asset of immeasurable worth, 'is an official of the Politburo of East Germany.' I looked again at his friend, at his brown, serious eyes and for an instant I saw the offspring of a dutiful high-ranking Communist. The story was implausible enough to be true. Only a month before, when hitch-hiking near Turin, I had been picked up by two young Hungarians, a laconic pair who had driven their battered Skoda across the Apennines in the grip of a ferocious death wish. One was a teacher, the other a journalist. They told me that they were both members of the Hungarian Communist Party and presented me with their Party cards when I showed scepticism.

'And now,' said Jan, getting up from the café table, 'we will leave you to recover your strength, so that you may once again follow your national calling.'

'Thanks.'

'The island is not so big. The privacy of the Anglo-Saxon cannot always be guaranteed,' he added cryptically. 'Ciao!' I watched them make their way along the quay, Jan's hand on Klaus's shoulder, until they disappeared among the ochre hulls of upturned fishing boats.

In the evening I ate alone in a restaurant hung about with glass floats and fishing nets. Fastened to the walls were the remains of unnameable sea creatures, their bones gleaming in the candlelight from the tables. I had failed to charm the waiter with my crude Italian, the food was unexciting and as consolation I was nearing the bottom of a litre of red wine. I thought back over my Italian grand tour, the three months that were drawing to an end, and the images of a hundred towns unreeled themselves in my imagination, the memories of some already blurring a little . . . was it Vicenza or Cremona where I had seen a hearse run out of control in a crowded street? And the *pensione* where a tiny monkey had answered the door to guests—was that Siena or Perugia? I recalled a long train journey to Naples, of being immobilised in the aisle of a shabby carriage with peasants taking produce to the city, wicker baskets and bundles of vegetables, white hens rocking with the movement of the train, their heads in fitted black hoods like condemned men . . . had I ever felt more free than on that train journey?

Behind me, near the door of the restaurant, I heard a commotion, voices arguing in German and then the unmistakable high laughter, a little drunken this time. I turned to see Jan threading his way among the tables. With him was Klaus, and behind them a slim woman with Slavonic features and closely cropped hair.

'Excuse us again,' said Jan. 'Please meet our friend Krista who after all did not drown in the harbour this morning.' The woman smiled a taut smile. She looked angry. Jan went on, 'Now we have the chance to celebrate this lack of a tragedy. We must buy you a drink.' Klaus, who was already drunk, but who still managed to look very serious, called the waiter over and ordered another bottle of wine.

'Una bottiglia grande,' he said with a large gesture. 'Una bottiglia rosso, alto, rotondo e profondo.'

Jan eyed him speculatively. 'When Klaus is drunk he likes to become the great Latin poet,' he said. Then, turning to me, 'We were having a small disagreement between friends. We need the views of someone who is unbiased.' Krista said something succinct in German that could have been obscene. Jan raised his hands in mock defence and grinned.

'Let me explain to you what has happened,' he said. Some time earlier the three of them have met a couple of Italians in a bar. The Italians, who appear to be very wealthy, are *en route* from Genoa to the Adriatic and their yacht is at present moored in the harbour. After an hour in the bar together the Italians excuse themselves, but invite their new friends to visit them later at the yacht, explaining that there is no shortage of room on the vessel and that they are welcome to stay overnight if they wish. It is apparent that one of the men has taken a fancy to Jan, and there is a suggestion that a little cocaine may become available.

'You see now the terrible temptations that are placed before the loyal Party member when he is abroad?' said Jan.

Krista broke in. 'So, another little joke. Let me guess that Jan has told you we are from East Berlin, perhaps also that Klaus is the son of the Party Secretary. But he has told these Italians that he and Klaus are the heirs to a West German newspaper empire and has invited them to visit him in the family villa on Lake Geneva. Unfortunately none of these things are true.'

Jan did not seem at all embarrassed by this disclosure. He spoke sadly to his wine glass.

'Krista can always bring the free spirit back to the earth when it thinks to fly too far away.' Then he looked up. 'It is good to try on other skins, don't you think?' I said that I didn't think it was too harmful. I was annoyed at myself for having believed Jan in the first place.

'We still have the problem of whether to visit these wealthy Italians and help them use up their expensive drugs,' said Jan. Krista said flatly that she was not going and Jan ordered another bottle of wine. While he was arguing over the price with the waiter, Krista told me that all three of them were students in West Berlin and that they had been coming to Lipari every summer for four years. By the time we finished the wine, Jan and Klaus had decided that they would take up the yachtsmen's invitation

When they had gone, Krista and I faced each other a little awkwardly across the table. I asked her why Klaus seemed to get more gloomy the more he drank.

'Klaus is like that. Also he's trying to have a relationship with a girl here in Lipari. This would make anyone depressive. Even in these times the fathers of Sicily keep their daughters locked up like wild dogs.' She got up from the table. 'We must go. Soon the hostel will be closing for the night.'

The hostel lay in a Venetian fortress overlooking the bay. It was approached through a tangle of narrow streets that ran down to the harbour. At night, the streets all looked similar, and this fact, combined with the effects of the wine, made us unsure of our direction. Krista told me about her eyesight, which at present was reasonably good. She suffered from a condition which badly affected her vision during a severe attack, but whose name she did not know in English. She was explaining what brought on the attacks when I realised we were lost, and by the time we had retraced our steps and followed the correct route, the heavy doors of the hostel were closed. The institution was run by a sandy-haired Italian whose moods fluctuated according to invisible laws: when I first arrived he was exceptionally friendly; however, earlier that day he had been curt and scowling, and now as we banged on the great studded doors I was apprehensive of what we might provoke in him. In the event there was no response from inside, the hostel remained dark and silent.

Part of the grounds of the fortress were marked off as an archaeological site, and as the night was warm and still, it occurred to me that this might be the safest place to sleep.

'How do you feel about spending the night among the bones of medieval Sicilians?'

Krista shrugged. 'Dead Sicilians I don't mind so much. It's when they are alive that I have problems with them.'

I looked into the inky digging, obscurely offended on behalf of a people I had not yet got to know and among whose ancestors I was about to bed down.

'Why bother to come here at all then?'

Krista was silent, and then she said, 'The difficulties for women—Klaus's friend for example—and for myself when I was travelling, perhaps they make me too cynical.'

We made our way cautiously through a series of linked pits, until we found what appeared to be a sheltered part of the digging. We lay on our backs looking up at the opaque Mediterranean night while Krista spoke of her journey through mainland Sicily. She said that she had spent several weeks in the mountainous interior, where she had stayed in 'thirsty villages containing only doves and old men'. She described the countryside of the interior, its bluffs and barren valleys, its scattering of lemon and lime trees, fixed in their places in the harsh soil by an unrelenting sun.

It had begun to get cold, so we pressed together for warmth, and some time that night, with the accumulated history of Lipari laid bare but invisible in the darkness around us, Krista and I became lovers, although my memory of how this happened, or which of us initiated events, is not at all clear. I woke in the morning to a fine rain falling on my face. Krista lay huddled against the wall of the pit. Between us were dislodged wooden markers, and I was wondering how far we had set back local archaeological research in our blind stumblings of the night before, when Krista sat up abruptly and looked around her.

'*Scheisse*. I'm soaking with water. Why are we sleeping in this stupid place?' She was looking at me with genuine anger. I wondered whether she had drunk more than I realised, and was beginning to remind her of our attempt to get into the hostel, when she got up, rubbed her eyes furiously with her fists and walked off through the site in the direction of the hostel. By the time I arrived in the lobby she had disappeared. The sandy-haired Italian watched me without curiosity as I signed the register in a hand so damp that the violet ink ran all over the page.

I lie on a blinding pumice beach. Nothing moves and I let the light seep through to the shuttered eyeball. With my fingers I penetrate the skin of pumice until I touch the damp layer below, the first rain that has fallen on Lipari in four months, the rain that despite its warmth and lightness has apparently so upset Krista. Now, after the morning clouds have cleared, the day is very hot, and ten metres away the Tyrrhenian Sea meets the pumice in a train of benevolent slaps. I am expecting the Berliners, who have told me that because of its seclusion this beach is their favourite on the island.

Jan's laugh announces their arrival from some distance off. He is with Krista and they wave at me across the dazzling pumice. Jan looks unusually pleased with himself and Krista too seems to have cheered up since the morning.

'Good, good,' said Jan, squatting beside me and inspecting me approvingly. 'You are getting some colour on your sad pale body.' With the deft movements of practised sunbathers, Jan and Krista took off their clothes, folded them carefully and stretched out naked beside me. Jan settled into the pumice and let out a contented sigh.

'It is only the sun that can purify the body after the sins of the night,' he said.

After an appropriate pause, I asked, 'How were the Italians?'

'The Italians were very interesting. If all the people of Genoa are like these Italians then Genoa must be a very decadent place. Perhaps next year I will go to visit this city and its wonderful people.'

'First, however, you must entertain them at your villa on Lake Geneva,' said Krista.

Jan laughed his brilliant laugh. 'You're right, honey. First I must do that.' He took out a tube of lotion and began to rub the almond-scented liquid into his skin.

'For Klaus, the night was not so good,' he said. 'Klaus is drinking to forget the girl who is shut away from him in the evenings. After a little more wine, Klaus became very excited and made his big speech about the barbarian fathers of Italy, using much foul language. Fortunately when Klaus is excited his Italian is not so good, and I think our hosts did not fully understand this speech. However, they understand when he lies down on the floor of their expensive yacht and vomits his stomach into their carpet.'

'And after all this, they still believed you were the sons of a wealthy publishing family?' I asked.

'But of course,' said Jan seriously. 'This is absolutely correct behaviour for the sons of wealthy newspaper families.'

Krista pulled a face. 'It's also absolutely normal behaviour for Klaus,' she said. She got up and picked her way gingerly across the hot pumice to the sea. She stood in the shallows with the water lapping around her ankles.

Jan called to her. 'Honey, your string is hanging down.' Krista half turned towards us, looked down and then tucked her tampon string up between her legs. Jan went on, 'And if you go into the water leaking out blood you will attract all the sharks of Africa to this beach.'

Krista picked up a piece of pumice from the shoreline and

109

threw it at him, the way boys are taught to throw, with a flick of the whole arm. Although the projectile had been aimed casually, it only narrowly missed Jan's head. Then Krista waded into the water and swam out into the bay with flat, even strokes. I told Jan that I thought he deserved to have been hit. He gave me a mocking smile.

'But you are such a gentleman.' He propped himself up on one elbow. 'You see, Krista and I have known each other for a very long time, since we were twelve years old in fact. At that time we made some sexual experiments with each other. However, these experiments were not so successful . . . ' He trailed off, and for a moment I thought he was expecting me to offer my commiserations. 'Since this time we have been very close,' he continued. 'But we no longer allow sex to make any complications in our relationship.'

I lay on my back, absorbing the heat from the pumice, trying to imagine the desultory coupling of twelve-year-olds in that distant grey city, trying to picture Jan and Krista growing up in a place that existed for me only as a collection of newsreel images, and I felt an irrational wave of depression at the unimaginable difference of our childhoods.

Jan was saying, ' . . . when Krista's eyesight began to cause problems, some very sensitive doctors told her that she could be starting to go blind. This is a particularly stupid thing to tell an angry person of sixteen years old. On this occasion, Krista also did something very stupid . . . ' He trailed off again, as though concerned that he was being indiscreet, then said abruptly, 'Berlin in the winter is a city with great dangers for the soul.'

Krista was swimming back from the headland towards the beach. Several times, involuntarily, I caught myself searching the bay for moving shadows beneath the surface.

'This is our fourth year of coming to Lipari,' Jan said. 'We have some kind of *affaire* with this island, Klaus, Krista and myself. Perhaps it is the strange *affaire* of Germany and Italy, which has been going on for a long time now. In the winter of Berlin I dream of lying on this beach and watching Krista swimming in the green water, and of arguing with Klaus about his crazy lusting for the girl who is locked away.'

'Klaus has been after the same girl all this time?'

Jan nodded. 'Each year it is the same. Sometimes I think that Klaus was born to be the sadist to himself.' He looked down at his own perfectly tanned body and frowned, as though baffled by the sheer perversity of Klaus's obsession. 'I tell him to lust instead for the Italian boys, who are not locked away at all.'

Krista had come up from the water and was standing beside us, drying her shock of blond hair and listening to our conversation. Her laugh was muffled by the towel.

'And when you and this wealthy yachtsman from Genoa are lusting for each other, what is his friend the other yachtsman doing?' she said.

Jan smiled. 'He's getting a little jealous, perhaps. However, he is much older, and some of his hairs are falling out, so he must be careful not to drive his friend away into the arms of some beautiful young man.'

'Like yourself, perhaps,' said Krista.

'Honey, you are very kind.'

In the evening the three of us went to the bar where Jan had first met the Italians. A little while later they walked in, dressed in immaculate white and with cashmere sweaters knotted casually about their necks. The younger of the two, Fabio, a languid youth with long eyelashes and an easy laugh, quickly joined Jan in a joking conversation concerning Klaus's misadventures on the yacht. Jan explained with transparent condescension that Klaus was out on another of his doomed missions at that very moment. Krista and I, who had avoided saying anything significant to each other all day, sipped vermouths and listened to the conversation. The Italians seemed charmingly straightforward and I wondered whether the decadence that Jan had spoken of was another of his compulsive inventions.

Eneri, a well-preserved man with the manner of a successful academic (he appeared to be Fabio's senior by at least fifteen years), even gave the impression of being progressive in his politics. As the evening wore on he spent some time explaining the tenacity of the Mafia in Sicily in terms of the protection given it by the right-wing political establishment. Jan, who was still playing up to his role as scion of the West German ruling classes, and who in any case was in competition with Eneri for the affections of his young friend, disagreed with his analysis, at first quite politely and then, when Eneri persisted, with a passion that became almost comical. It was undeniable, Jan declared, that the only serious threat to the Mafia had been during the Mussolini years, when Il Duce's man in Palermo had been unafraid to treat the families with proper savagery, to the point of throwing the wives and children of prominent Mafiosi into jail.

Eneri said mildly that the years of fascism had been a special case and that he had been speaking of the political establishment since the war.

Jan gripped his glass and sat up straight in his chair. 'So you think that fascism was a special case in the history of your country. This is also what Germans would like to believe . . . ' Krista laid a hand on his arm. She spoke to the Italians as though excusing the behaviour of a brilliant child.

'Jan is an enthusiastic student of these matters, and it's dangerous to start on such discussions with him. Unless of course you're keen to hear about the whole of your history since the time of Garibaldi.'

Eneri said that he would be very interested to hear such an account of Italy's history, but perhaps, yes, it would be better to leave it for another occasion. Jan was not going to be deterred so easily. His pupils seemed unnaturally dilated and he spoke very fast.

'Perhaps you believe it's better that we push these things into a dark corner of the mind. Of course the Germans and Italians are afraid to look too hard at this part of their history. We like to think that the fascists were just very clever men who fooled the people with their brilliant propaganda.'

I said, 'Surely that's partly tr . . . '

Jan cut in. 'It is a lie. Fascism grew up within the culture of

112

the nation. Our parents and grandparents have spent forty years trying to pretend this is not so. They prefer to believe that they were fooled by the evil genius of Goebbels and Hitler. Until they accept that they were guilty, the soul of Germany will stay with its poison.'

Fabio, who had given the appearance of being bored by the conversation, carefully inspected his fingernails and said that this might be true of Germany, but he did not think it was true of Italy. I was surprised by Jan's outburst, and it had clearly not endeared him to the Italians, who not long afterwards made their excuses and wandered off.

We sat at the bar in silence for some time. And then Jan said, 'This may be the last we see of the wealthy yachtsmen from Genoa.'

I ordered Jan another drink and Krista said, 'Think of the difficulties if you had fallen in love with Fabio.'

'Perhaps I have already fallen in love with Fabio,' said Jan with unconvincing defiance.

Krista linked her arm in mine. 'And perhaps I have fallen in love too.'

Jan looked from one to the other of us, visibly shocked. 'Is this true?'

'Of course it's not true. We have only known each other for a day or so.'

Jan smiled a wan smile, but he had already begun to look more cheerful. 'Honey, you should not play jokes at such moments.'

Krista and I spent a lot of time together in the next few days, although our previous intimacy was not discussed. We went on long walks on the deserted coastal roads, we passed the pumice quarries on the northern end of the island, their monolithic hoppers, mobile gantries and vaulted conveyer chains functioning without any sign of human intervention. A pall of white pumice dust hung over this end of the island, as though the land was throwing up a veil in order to decently obscure the violence being done to its geological heart. Often we walked in silence, intruders in a scene of studied monochrome, the sky empty of birds and the sea leaden and subdued.

In this part of the island, autumn in northern Europe did not seem so far away, and Krista talked of her return to Berlin, of the claustrophobia that overcame the city in winter, and of the deterioration of her eyesight that followed the cold.

'The problem with Berlin,' she said, 'is that there is no escape from the past. When Jan says the Germans refuse to look at their history, he's correct, but in Berlin itself we have the opposite problem. Everywhere we go we encounter the past—in the form of a snake of concrete that runs through our city. So Berlin also has its sickness. Too much of this past is as bad as too little.'

We had come to a headland at the end of the island and the path we had been following ended suddenly before a long drop to the sea. I said to Krista that in Polynesia such places were considered to be stepping-off points for spirits on their way to the underworld. We looked over the sea to the spectral shapes of the outlying islands and I considered the idea that this anonymous piece of ocean was eventually continuous with the vivid Pacific.

Krista said, 'You're very lucky to come from a country which is too young to have the problems of Germany.'

'We have our own nightmares from the past,' I said. 'A country as far from anywhere as mine finds it easier to keep these nightmares secret.'

'I think these are quite small nightmares, in comparison.' Krista was standing near the edge of the bluff watching a boat at the base of the rocks. Far below, two men were lifting lobster pots from the sea. She moved a little closer to the edge, perhaps to obtain a better view of the fishermen.

'I like your story of departing spirits,' she said. 'As a spirit I would feel privileged to leave from this point.'

She was at the very edge of the cliff now, and she raised a finger to her lips as though listening for the sighs of departing wraiths. But it was very quiet up there on the bluff, and the only sound that broke the silence was the disembodied slap of oars from the base of the rocks.

114

Krista stepped back from the edge, threw her arms around my neck and cried,

'Today the spirits are staying at home!'

Making love in the white dust of an abandoned valley, Krista talked of the spirits she had listened to the last time we had been together, spirits that hummed in the chambers of the digging below the fortress. She told me she had stayed awake half that night while the history of the place had risen up around us in the dark. Now, moving together in the white dust, she talked of Arabs and Venetians, invaders who had come to the islands across the millennia, who had settled and died here, and whose bodies now fertilised the earth beneath us. Fucking and talking like this, she said, was a medicine, but when I whispered 'For what sickness?' she wouldn't answer me. Wraiths ourselves, with the pumice dust sticking to our skins, we followed the valley to a beach and washed it away in the dull sea.

Later, in a crowded café in the main town, Krista covered her eyes with a hand and spoke softly to herself in German. When I asked her what was wrong, she answered irritably, still in German, and wouldn't explain further. Jan and Klaus were consoling themselves with drink that evening, Klaus for the usual reasons, and Jan in preparation for the departure of his yachtsmen, who had been seen preparing their vessel for sailing. We sat on the terrace of a bar that overlooked the main harbour, while Jan and Klaus sang sentimental German folk-songs and we drank from the neck of a bottle of grappa.

'By next summer,' said Klaus, his voice thick with the grappa, 'I think this barbarian father will have forced his daughter to marry a Sicilian boy.'

Jan put an arm round his shoulders. 'This is very serious. We must look for another girl immediately. Without this lusting it is impossible to imagine a proper summer on Lipari.' Klaus shook his head and muttered that this girl was irreplaceable, he would go mad before he could forget her . . .

Jan passed me the grappa. 'You see now the optimism of the

true native of Berlin.' I asked Klaus whether he had considered running away with the girl. He peered at me, bleary-eyed.

'That is out of the question,' he said with bleak finality.

Jan said, 'The barbarian father might arrange for the Mafia to search out the fleeing couple.' He seemed to savour the sheer infamy of the idea. Since the argument with the yachtsmen, speculation on the influence of the Mafia had been a regular feature of conversation. We spent some time discussing elaborate plans for releasing the girl from captivity and ruses for throwing the Mafia off the trail.

At last Klaus broke in. 'This is quite stupid. She would never agree to such crazy ideas.'

Krista shrugged. 'Then perhaps you're wasting your time with this girl.'

'However, we can't just abandon her to the savage father,' said Jan.

'If she won't consider escape,' said Krista, 'perhaps she's not so keen on this romance as you believe.'

Jan eyed her reproachfully. 'Honey, that is most unkind.'

Krista shrugged again. 'Perhaps it's time for Klaus to wake up from his dream.' Suddenly she sounded very angry. 'Perhaps it's time for all of us to wake up. Fantasies about the character of the Latins. Dreams of the beautiful Italians who can save us from ourselves. Is this how we are going to spend the rest of our lives?'

Jan bit his lip. 'So. Everything is clear. Italy is no longer good for us. The playing ground has been closed off. Next summer we will all make love to New Zealanders.' In an attempt to retrieve the situation, I tried a feeble joke.

'I'm afraid we only make love above certain altitudes.' But Jan and Krista were no longer listening.

'Why do we come here year after year?' said Krista. 'So we can gaze at the Italians and pretend to have exotic romances? Unfortunately these romances are always dead before they are born.'

Jan sat rigid in his chair. 'And of course you will be able to tell us why this is the case.'

Krista slammed her glass down on the table, her face suddenly ugly with despair.

'Are you so stupid that you can't see it for yourself?' Her movement had upset the bottle of grappa, and now it spun across the table and shattered on the tiles at our feet. We sat there immobilised, while the creamy dusk descended over the sea and settled among the cane tables and chairs of the bar. And then Krista was on her feet and away down the path from the terrace, while the rest of us sat and watched the dregs of the grappa disappear between the black and white tiles.

I looked for Krista at the hostel and at the bars in town. Then I checked the port area and the arms of the piers enclosing the harbour. I took the road along the coast, pausing to check the beach where we had gone to sunbathe. At dusk this part of the island was even more desolate and at intervals along the road, like the desiccated victims of a drought, stood the spindly shapes of prickly pears. Now I was half walking, half running. I passed the valley where we had made love in the white dust of pumice, past the remains of a boat beached far beyond the shoreline by an invisible hand, until eventually I approached the headland at the end of the island.

I could imagine now the sighs of wraiths, the whispers converging in a susurration that thickened the dusk. Krista's Arabs and Venetians, the foreigners who had voyaged to these islands down the ages, and whose histories of colonisation and death had returned to obsess her . . . I heard them as they rose on the air and flooded out towards that high point overlooking the sea. I was caught up among them now myself, impelled towards the headland on a tide of whispers that had taken on the strength of a steady breeze. I ran up the path that led from the road to the bluff and cast around in the half darkness. There was no sign of Krista. I called into the dusk, but my voice was snatched away by the eddies that moved swiftly over the headland. At the edge of the bluff I looked down to where the ocean sucked and drew on the rocks . . . but the light was fading now and the jumble of granite withdrew into the gloom. I stood there on the top of the bluff while a dark wind carrying the

117

memories of Krista's labyrinthine fears blew past me on its way out to the horizon.

When the sea had turned black, I walked down the path to the road. The air was still, the whispers had faded with the light, and I walked in a cocoon of silence along the road towards the lights of the town. The effects of the grappa had worn off, and I felt dull and stripped of emotion. I passed the moonscape of the pumice quarries, their stark architecture pitched up against the night sky. Whatever happened, I knew that my time in Italy was over, and that I would leave the islands as soon as possible.

Krista was sitting on a sand-dune near the road, and I would have missed her in the gloom if she hadn't called out as I went by. Her voice seemed unnaturally loud. She said that she had been on her way to the headland when her eyesight and the failing light had prevented her going on. She had watched me pass from the dunes above the beach. I had looked very grim, she said, and smiled. I stood there for a while in silence, thinking of the headland at dusk, and of the metallic sea that stretched away to the coast of Africa. Then she held out a hand, and I pulled her to her feet. 'Why don't you come and stay in Berlin for a while?' she said.

We walked arm in arm towards the lights of the town, while images from an old newsreel turned in my mind: women cleaning bricks among blackened churches, the Reichstag against a white sky . . . barbed wire, airlifts and the sluggish river Spree.

HUIA AND THE ANGRY EARTH

IT WAS THE RAIN of green plums that woke Huia to the realisation that something was wrong with the world. A passing kaka looked down at the stirring girl as the plums fell about her as hard and cold as hail-stones. By the time the kaka had swooped to blunt its beak on the unyielding fruit, Huia was sitting upright and looking around at the trees of the convent orchard performing a mad dance in the agitated soil.

She watched with puzzlement as the water in the creek beyond the plum trees stopped flowing, reversed its direction, and began to move up the bed in the direction of the mountains. Eels, as surprised as Huia, churned the water in protest at the reversal of thousand-year-old certainties. Nothing was still, and even the breeze took on the guise of a maddened spirit. As the last of the fruit were shaken from the dancing trees, Huia was up and running towards the seductive stillness of the distant ranges.

The dusty main street of her village was deserted as she passed through on her way to the mountains. Next morning, after a fearful night in a ditch beside the road, she returned to the town, exhausted and barely able to walk. The hands of the shattered town clock hung down to greet her and the streets were thick with smells released from the bowels of the earth. At the convent, where she had laboured for three years over inexplicable books, the walls were in ruins and the windows watched her with blind, glassless eyes. Sheep from the convent farm now wandered through the class-rooms and nibbled at the discarded showers of kaleidoscopic chalk. Huia sat in an empty class-room amongst the morbid flappings of abandoned books, and thought about the beginning of the end of the world. Then she got up and tried on a nun's habit. Clad in black, and hoisting the lower hem of her new garment like a princess, she searched the institution for food to satisfy her growing hunger. She found unexpectedly rich pickings in the living quarters of the Mother Superior. Gorged on tinned delicacies from Europe, and drunk on Wairarapa mead, she fell asleep beneath a pew in the Chapel of Our Lady where she had gone to thank the Blessed Virgin for sparing her from the outrageous movements of the earth.

She woke to the noxious breath and insistent tongue of a sheep from the convent farm. Without a trace of shame, the flock had now occupied the chapel, and were grazing on the lush adornments of the altar. Embroidered hangings from the transept had been pulled to the floor and chewed until they were threadbare. Moved by the composure and enterprise of the animals, Huia searched among the cupboards behind the altar and laid out wafers and wine for the sheep before the communion rail. Clad in her oversized habit, and intoning the dimly remembered Latin Mass as she ministered to the animals, it occurred to her that occasional movements of the earth might not be such a terrible thing after all.

Through the remarkable evidence people leave of their lives when fleeing from earthquakes, Huia learnt more of human nature in the next few days than she had in her preceding thirteen years. By nature a dreamy person, her knowledge of the secrets of the adult world was acquired during innocent forays for food in the wreckage of the convent, rather than through any desire to pry. She learnt, for example, that Sister Eustace collected Elvis Presley records in astounding numbers, which she stored in butter boxes behind stacks of bottled peaches at the back of a massive wardrobe. Aside from Mother Superior's taste in tinned Camembert, she was also partial to Dutch cigars, a taste that Huia herself was quick to acquire, though she was almost as fond of the gentle fragrance of the sandalwood boxes in which they were kept.

The convent was located outside the town, and two days later she made her first trip into the centre for supplies. Her suspicion that the town would remain evacuated for some time was confirmed by the crack that had opened up along the length of the main street, and which gave off the sulphurous smells and superheated gases of Whakarewarewa. After lecturing the convent sheep on the dangers of the wound in the earth (since their holy induction they had followed her everywhere), Huia tucked up her flowing habit, mounted the steps to the upper veranda of the only hotel and took stock of the scene below. Little of the town was undamaged and most of the shops along the main street were exposed to the elements through their shattered front windows. Water mains had burst and were flooding the gutters and pavements, and power poles teetered dangerously above the ruptured earth. From the high wooden veranda, Huia issued a proclamation declaring herself the interim mayor of the town and its environs, and extending to herself certain important powers until proper administration could be restored. On the street below, the flock of Holy Sheep watched in respectful silence while she smoked an inaugural cigar over the scene of municipal desolation.

Under her newly announced powers, Huia was able with clear conscience to obtain the supplies she required, and was returning to the convent with her flock when she came upon a prostrate figure, dragging itself down the main street towards the wound in the earth with the terrible strength of an intending suicide. Awed by the conviction in his expression, Huia watched in silence until his strength began to fail some fifty metres or so from the fulminous crack. Then she asked the motionless figure why, after having survived the earthquake, he was now so intent on dying in its aftermath.

'Life for a cripple in this town will be hell,' murmured the dusty figure and began to crawl again. Despite her religious training, Huia felt no particular horror at the notion of suicide. She was certain, however, that the cripple was wrong to be so pessimistic, and with the dignity of her newly acquired position and the force of her compassionate nature, she spoke convincingly against his decision to end his life. Too slight to help him walk, Huia informed the prostrate figure that she would return with the tractor and trailer from the convent farm, and that in the meantime she would leave a contingent of her Holy Sheep to watch over him. Two days later, when Huia had still

121

not returned and even the Holy Sheep were beginning to get restless, the cripple lapsed once more into profound gloom, and began again his painful progress through the dust. The flaw in Huia's plan had been to assume that someone who had never driven a vehicle before could learn in an hour or so, a belief brought about by the intoxication of newly assumed high office.

On her first attempt to master the ancient vehicle, her outsized habit caught in the axle of the rear wheels and flung her to the ground with the force of a hurricane. Humiliated and bruised, her determination redoubled, she remounted the tractor with the habit knotted at her waist. On this occasion she had gone no more than fifty metres when the tractor slid into a ditch, where it remained firmly lodged. Despairing of her efforts to free the vehicle, Huia returned to the town with food for the cripple, only to find the abyss now threatening to engulf the entire main street, and the cripple about to throw himself off its edge. Reprimanding the fickle guard of sheep (who had yet to learn the discipline of their calling and had retreated in cowardice to the lower veranda of the hotel), Huia dragged the suicide back from the edge of the crack and found him shelter in the gutted shell of the corner bakery.

At Eucharist that evening in the chapel of Our Lady of the Sheep, the mayor-shepherdess and her flock prayed for guidance in the matter of the stranded vehicle. After entering a trance-like state of grace, during which Huia dispensed the Holy Sacraments with unearthly calm, she withdrew to a lectern in the transept and began to write instructions of great complexity in an exercise book. The following morning, with the help of a pestle and mortar, ingredients from the ruined convent kitchen and strips of sheet torn from Sister Eustace's bed, a mysterious preparation was applied to the rear wheels of the tractor as a series of poultices. Exactly what contribution this preparation made to the rescue will never be known, but when Huia threw the stranded machine into reverse gear, a team of Holy Sheep yoked and straining at the rear axle, it flew from the ditch without further difficulty and Lewis the cripple was brought from the stricken town to take up safer quarters in the ruins of the convent.

The victim of an illness that had withered his right leg in childhood, Lewis had spent the intervening years in a relentless programme of self-education. Denied access to the world around him like other children he had also developed a potent sensitivity to smell. Now, quartered in the ruined kitchen, he spoke of the scents of a thousand convent meals, details of which he could pluck out of the air with an accuracy that left Huia silent with admiration. He told of the Easter lunch that the nuns had eaten some weeks before, the smell of which had penetrated the brickwork of the convent, and had now been released by the catastrophe of the earthquake. He spoke of a generous leg of mutton, basted with French mustard and ringed with fresh Brussels sprouts, and was beginning his description of the dessert when the Holy Sheep set up a chorus of displeasure and prevented him from going on. Made bold by their liberation from the convent farm and their elevation to holy status, the sheep had developed strongly vegetarian instincts, and were offended by this talk of flesh-eating. Lewis, a student of the works of the anarchist Bakunin, was quick to assert that his description did not imply approval of what had been eaten. He explained how disagreement on the subject of flesh-eating had existed in the early anarchist movement, and had contributed in small part to the famous split between the followers of Bakunin and those of Proudhon. He was of the opinion that meat-eating was oppressive and hence anti-revolutionary, and he himself would be happy to survive on cheese and vegetables for the rest of his life. Huia listened to all this with considerable interest, and at Eucharist that evening in the Chapel of Our Lady of the Sheep, consulted with the Holy Virgin on the subject of meat-eating, also seeking guidance on whether the Holy Sacraments were indeed the sanctified flesh and blood of the crucified Jesus. During the ecstasy of prayer she learned to her relief that such notions were abominations and distortions of true faith, and that the consumption of meat and meat products was, as Lewis had suggested, essentially anti-revolutionary and godless.

Armed with this revelation, which she announced to Lewis and the approving sheep next morning, Huia organised a collection of all fish and meat products remaining in the ruined convent and its environs. When they had retrieved the last corned beef from the convent kitchen, unearthed Mother Superior's cache of tinned Bluff oysters (this latter through Lewis's detective skills) and gathered up the rotting contents of the convent freezer, they loaded it all on the trailer of the Massey Ferguson and followed a jubilant vanguard of Holy Sheep into town. Water from the broken mains continued even now to wash down the main street, cascade into the abyss opened up by the earthquake and thunder out again like the superheated vents of Wairakei. At the edge of the abyss, shrouded in swirling steam, the procession came to a halt. Huia gave thanks for the revelation, then broke rice wafers over the abyss. Lewis stood up on the trailer with the aid of his crutch and recited a passage from early Bakunin with fluency and passion. (Such was the excitement of the Holy flock that one of the sheep plunged over the edge and disappeared forever, but because of the obscuring steam the tragedy was not discovered until some time later.) Huia and Lewis then consigned the forbidden foodstuffs to the abyss without further ceremony. The little procession returned to the convent in triumph with Huia venturing into top gear for the first time, Lewis waving his crutch aloft and the Holy Sheep following along behind.

Life in the ruined convent began to take on a regular pattern. In the mornings, Lewis held classes in algebra, the recognition of scents and the history of revolutionary thought. Although Huia was the main beneficiary of his learning, the Holy Sheep would often attend the more elementary lessons. Evenings centred on the ecstatic Eucharists of the mayor-shepherdess, in which the emerging doctrines of the commune were refined and adjusted through the revelations of the Blessed Virgin. At other times, Lewis and Huia explored the ruined town on the old tractor, sometimes taking major diversions to avoid the crack, which was still threatening to cut the town in two.

On the hilly north side they found houses they had never

realised existed, hidden away behind carefully pruned hedges and containing more rooms than they believed possible. Most of these houses were in ruins, shattered by the earthquake or carved in two by slips—a living room with its chaise longue looking out on the raw earth of a gully; a staircase leading nowhere; a refrigerator perched in an elegant garden. Lewis, who rarely missed an opportunity to quote the great anarchists, surveyed the opulent interiors of these gutted houses from the trailer and declared in his resonant voice, 'Property is theft'. Their appetites insatiable now that they had denied themselves meat products, Lewis and Huia plundered the houses for food. Lewis stood beneath fruit trees and vines snaring feijoas and passion-fruit with his crutch, while Huia explored the kitchens and pantries, sometimes directed to a hidden source of food by Lewis's olfactory gifts. Occasionally they came upon religious items—rosaries, crucifixes and sacred oleographs—which they carried off to the convent in order to further decorate the Chapel of Our Lady of the Sheep.

The morning classes turned to discussion of these elegant suburbs and the wealth they had found in the abandoned houses. Lewis spoke at length on the political economy of the town, laying bare the subtle workings of the dialectic and outlining the principles of historical materialism. The little commune began to develop a radical analysis of its environs, notable for its combination of anarchist and religious principles, and before long the classes turned to consideration of ways in which this analysis could be put into effect. The first thing they hit upon was the stockyards on the road into town.

An impressive, maze-like structure, which relied for its strength on posts of eight-inch totara, the stockyards had been untouched by the ravages of the earthquake, and symbolised for the Holy Sheep the very essence of the subjugation of beast by man. The following Sunday was the first of May, and the commune decided to mark their first May Day with the destruction of this monument of oppression. Throughout the week they worked to construct a harness large enough for the entire flock of Holy Sheep. Lewis studied the layout of the yards and identified the weak points in the structure. On the morning of the planned destruction the flock was marshalled on the road beside the stockyards, and the harness attached by heavy chains to the foundation posts. After a short prayer by Huia, Lewis propped himself up on the trailer and signalled the first charge with a bold sweep of his crutch. Disaster followed, as the totara posts withstood the shock and the harness parted under the strain. One of the Holy Sheep suffered a broken back and to the great distress of the commune had to be destroyed. That evening a sober Mass was held in the chapel, and afterwards Huia spent the night in restless turmoil, unable to sleep, the terrible cries of the injured sheep still ringing in her ears.

Before Mass the next evening Huia searched the trunks in the ruined quarters of the Mother Superior until she came upon a finely cut garment of cream and gold linen. Throwing off her old torn black habit, she donned the ceremonial robes of the ancient nun, and experienced a mysterious lightness flooding through her body. From its fragrant sandalwood box Huia took the very last of the Dutch cigars, which she smoked with savour and a deep sense of regret. Thus prepared for the Eucharist, she entered the chapel where the little commune was patiently assembled. Bent before the altar and inhaling deeply on the thick fumes from the incense burner, Huia was drawn into ecstatic communion with the Holy Virgin in order to seek guidance on the problem of the intractable stockyards. Late that night, when the rest of the commune had gone to their makeshift sleeping quarters, Huia stole out along the road to the stockyards and glided like a luminous moth among the maze of pens and races, her ears tuned to the breathing of the ancient timbers.

The harness was repaired and another attempt made on the stockyards the following morning. As the Holy Sheep stood assembled in readiness for their renewed charge, Huia mounted the trailer once more and made a solemn announcement. It had been revealed to her, she declared, that it was not enough merely to destroy the fabric of the old order—it was also necessary to begin the construction of the new. The wood from the stockyards, she said, would be used in the construction of a grand new building to house the commune, a structure that would be perfectly circular in order to celebrate the principle of equality on which the commune had been founded. Roused to new heights of excitement by this speech, the Holy Sheep charged spontaneously in perfect unison and the stockyards, which had been mysteriously weakened overnight, disintegrated at once with a barely audible sigh.

Although the basic shape of the new building had come to Huia by revelation, there was much still to be done in matters of design, and to this end Lewis combed the wreckage of the town library for books on engineering and architecture. He then turned his formidable powers of scholarship to developing a set of drawings for the structure, which would be built beside the ruins of the convent and which they had decided to call Oranga. For many weeks Lewis was absorbed in the obscure world of load-bearing walls, shear-strengths and vaulted atria. Occasionally he would emerge from the ruined kitchen where he worked to issue an order for materials, and Huia and a contingent of sheep would go out and search among the ruins of the town.

They used the totara stakes of the stockyards to construct the frame of the house, and stripped iron from the slip-torn houses of the wealthy suburbs for the roof. By now they had run out of fuel for the tractor, and materials had to be dragged from the town with the harness and chains. Lewis's design called for a roof supported by beams radiating from a central column like the spokes of an umbrella, and it was during the delicate operation to secure these in place that the second earthquake struck. Since the catastrophe that had brought them all together, occasional tremors had shaken the town, provoking minor slips in the wealthy suburbs of the north and causing sulphurous gases to spill from the chasm in the main street. Because of the earthquake that had brought about their liberation, the commune had always looked upon the movement of the earth as their ally, and were unprepared for the second quake, despite the portent of a low-flying kaka that passed over the town heading north. The quake struck at noon on the day the last of the great roof beams was being lowered into place. A rending sound began in the bowels of the earth, and the ground stretched like a waking animal. From the hidden pores of the earth came the acrid gases of sleeping volcanoes and great clouds of dust obscured the horizon. The frame of the great building flexed like a bow; the roof-beams began to quiver, then plummeted to the ground, bringing disaster to the squad of sheep harnessed to the lifting tackle.

When the debris came to rest, twelve of the Holy Sheep lay crushed beneath the collapsing timbers. Lewis, who had been supervising the winching operation from inside the building, had a miraculous escape, which he attributed to his uncanny sense of smell. Seconds before the quake, a sudden premonition caused him to throw himself beneath a saw-horse, which took the impact of a falling beam and prevented his head being crushed like an egg. When Lewis extricated himself from the ruins of the building and limped to the chapel, Huia was seated in the aisle with the glazed and catatonic look of the newly speechless. She had observed the catastrophe from the window of the roofless chapel, and had been struck dumb by the slaughter of her comrades. For several days Lewis tried without success to penetrate the veil that had fallen over her eyes, and then he turned to the grim business of retrieving the bodies of the sheep from the ruins. Work on the building ceased, and grief enveloped the commune, which in a single stroke had lost a half of its members. Huia could not be roused from her stupor, and without their spiritual leader the commune was paralysed. Lewis spent many hours in the chapel, pleading with her to relinquish her guilt. No one could have foreseen the disaster, he said, it was on a scale far greater than what might be discovered through the ordinary business of revelation. But Huia could not be placated and after five days in the chapel she got up without a word, put on her old torn habit, and walked amongst the wreckage of the town. Although tears could be seen streaming down her face, she turned the sound of her grief inwards, so that she wept in absolute silence.

Huia's wanderings continued for several weeks, during which time she crossed the town forty-seven times. Only after this marathon of exercise had she dissipated her grief, but she never forgave herself for failing to predict the second earthquake and every Thursday thereafter she put on her old black habit in penance and mourning. Life in the commune gradually returned to normal, as the debris of the abortive building programme were cleared away, and Lewis went back to his drawings in an attempt to redesign the building so as to make it completely resistant to earthquake damage. The terrible loss of half their number drew the commune more tightly together, so that the evening Masses and morning classes had a new atmosphere of solidarity, and the inhabitants of the little commune began to acquire the mysterious habit of reading one another's thoughts. Knowledge could now be passed directly from one communard to another, so that speech began to be dispensed with and the morning classes took place in companionable silence.

In spite of his attachment to the beliefs of the nineteenth-century anarchists, Lewis became an enthusiastic participant in the Eucharist, to the point where he specially adapted a habit from the wardrobe of the absent Mother Superior in order to properly dress for his duties as chief acolyte to the mayor-shepherdess. Although denied the same visionary experiences as Huia, he was frequently able to help in their interpretation, and took great pleasure in ensuring the order of the Mass was followed correctly. Although Huia was still only fourteen, and Lewis six years older than that, they had both begun to acquire an ageless quality brought about by their struggles with nature and moral philosophy.

During his long drafting sessions in the ruined kitchen, Lewis developed a radical idea for the design of Oranga which he hoped would make it resistant to even the strongest earthquake. His plan was to rest the structure on floating foundations, and he laboriously constructed a working model of his proposal. It was agreed that Huia would obtain advice through revelation on the likely success of this novel scheme, and at Eucharist that evening the carefully constructed model was placed before the altar for inspection by the Blessed Virgin. In the course of the Eucharist Huia had it confirmed to her that the floating foundations, with slight but important modifications, were an ingenious and reliable protection against the ravages of earthquakes, and construction of the second Oranga began the next day.

With the immediacy of understanding that had come about through their new ability to read each other's thoughts, the commune made steady progress on the project, and the revolutionary floating foundations were completed by the end of the first week. Once more materials were gathered from the ruins of the stockyards and the slip-torn suburbs of the town and dragged to the convent, where they were incorporated into the growing structure under the technical guidance of Lewis and spiritual co-ordination of Huia. No detail of the plan was too small to escape Lewis's attention, and no stage too insignificant to go without the vigilant blessings of the mayor-shepherdess. Gradually the extraordinary building took shape, a great circular edifice that had no precedent in the region, and which even half-complete astonished them all with its grace and symmetry. The pagoda-style roof towered over the surrounding countryside, and could be seen from the farthest side of the town. Inside, the living quarters had been carefully planned on democratic principles, so that each member of the commune had a wedge of the building radiating from the centre, and no apartment was larger or more elaborate than any other. The study classes under Lewis's guidance had come to the conclusion that the history of revolutionary action was the history of acquiring the very best for the dispossessed, so sumptuous furnishings were stripped from the gaping houses of the suburbs in order to properly decorate the interior. When it was finally completed, Oranga was as palatial and well appointed as the most elaborate hill-top mansion. During the course of the construction, several after-shocks from the earthquake that had destroyed its predecessor rocked the structure, but Lewis's floating foundations absorbed the motion without difficulty, and while the land all about it shivered, Oranga remained stately, immobile and undamaged.

The commune planned a grand opening for the day of final completion, and preparations began for the great feast that would be the centre-piece of the celebrations. The Holy Sheep combed the town and countryside for delicacies that had escaped their previous foraging, and food was piled high on a massive trestle table set out in front of the building. Lewis, who had become a cook of impressive stature, concocted an astonishing variety of dishes from a limited number of ingredients, and seasoned them with the rare herbs he had learnt to cultivate in his ruined kitchen. Huia, whose unearthly tranquillity had been completely restored since the tragedy of the second earthquake, led a brief service of thanksgiving on the morning of the great feast, during which the entire commune took communion, but at which the Holy Virgin failed once more to provide warning of a new and terrible threat to the labours of the community.

They had all been so occupied with the completion of the building that they had failed to keep watch on the great chasm that had rent the town in two. Since the second earthquake the chasm had been lengthening by several metres every day, and now the great vents of steam were forcing the earth apart at greater speed. A lone Holy Sheep returning from an expedition for banqueting food in the furthest suburbs happened upon the crack at the moment it began to move up the road towards the convent. Behind the fleeing animal the chasm swallowed an orchard and moved on towards the remains of the stockyards without pausing. The terrified sheep ran quivering and exhausted into the grounds of the ruined convent and raised the alarm. For several minutes there was pandemonium among the assembled communards, who were on the point of beginning the first course of their celebratory banquet. Then Huia climbed up onto the table and raised her hands and within seconds utter calm had descended on the company. From where she stood Huia could see the last of the derelict stockyards disappearing into the maw of the chasm, which stretched back now through the town and as far as the eye could see. After three Hail Marys and seven genuflections she turned her mind to the rituals of the Eucharist. Again she felt the mysterious lightness flooding through her limbs and on this occasion the watching commune observed a slight but distinct glow surrounding the slender figure in its magnificent gold and cream habit. To the communards she appeared momentarily to spin like a top, but the movement was so rapid that those observing were unsure whether they had been victims of a trick of the light. And then their attention was distracted by acrid vapours of sulphur, which marked the imminent arrival of the great crack. Huia was deep now in the thrall of her trance: in rapid succession she saw the rain of green plums that heralded the first earthquake, the rainbow showers of chalk in the ruined class-rooms, the fallen beams of the first Oranga . . . and she knew in that instant that it was within her grasp to prevent the destruction of the commune they had struggled so hard to build. The light surrounding the shepherdess sharpened in intensity and in her vision Huia penetrated to the forces deep in the heart of the earth, and she sensed the terrible strength of the processes that had been sculpting the face of the land. It seemed to her then that the land was in revolt against its violation by past custodians, against the abuse of its bounty and the plunder of its forests, and with the irresistible force of youthful enlightenment she made a solemn pledge on behalf of Lewis and the surviving Holy Sheep that from then on the commune would dedicate itself to the harmonious use of the land and its riches, and that anything they took from the land would be replaced in full. Miraculously, the acrid gases turned to the pungent scent of ripening fruit, and the great wound in the earth closed up with a clap that echoed among the distant hills for many hours afterwards.

The communards looked on in stupor at the transformation of the landscape and at the luminous figure with the grace and serenity of a saint who nonetheless had to lift the hem of her outsized habit in order to avoid tripping as she stepped down from the table. Then Lewis, who was not at all renowned for his gaiety, got up and began to dance among the dishes of his own preparation, and the Holy Sheep set up a chorus of jubilation that mixed with the echoes of the thunderclap to produce a fearsome sound, which in turn began a chaotic and tumultuous celebration that continued beyond sunrise the following morning and long beyond the sunset after that.

The book you have been reading is part of Heinemann Reed's Pacific Writers Series, a show-case for the finest fiction from New Zealand and the Pacific Islands. Details of some of the other titles available are given below, but for further information please write to: Pacific Writers Series, Heinemann Reed, Private Bag, Birkenhead, Auckland 10.

EARTHLY DELIGHTS
Nick Hyde

Michael Jones was an artist; now he paints houses. Greta Wolffsky was a famous actress; now she is undergoing 'treatment'. When Michael meets Greta in small-town New Zealand, he is shaken from the comfortable vacuum his life has become and forced to confront the ghosts of his past. It is a confrontation that leads to joy, enchantment, despair, and ultimately bloodshed.

Earthly Delights, Nick Hyde's first novel, combines comedy and pathos with a rare lightness of touch. Moving from the smoky conviviality of Amsterdam to the rough-hewn insularity of rural 'Puapiro', it is an absorbing tale underpinned by a belief in the value of good story-telling. The major characters are engagingly credible, and in Nelson—redundant journalist, inebriate and Rabelaisian raconteur—the author has created one of the funniest figures in New Zealand fiction.

'This is an immensely readable piece of writing, with excellent characterisation and the best evocation I have read of Amsterdam . . . There is no doubt that the author is a committed and able writer.' MICHAEL GIFKINS

THE FRIGATE BIRD
Alistair Campbell

'*The Frigate Bird* is a fabulous blend of Cook Island and *papa'a* ways of seeing. It is a map that only Alistair Campbell—with his unique imagination as a poet and visionary traveller through Pacific cultures—could have drawn.' ALBERT WENDT

This, Alistair Campbell's first novel, is as rich and compelling as the poetry for which he is well known. Set partly in the Cook Islands, partly in a New Zealand psychiatric hospital, and partly within the confines of the narrator's mind, it is about a search—for love, sanity and the innocence of childhood. Along the way, it introduces some of the most bizarre and colourful characters to have appeared in Pacific fiction: Big Mouth, the Minotaur, Mr Soo, and the demonic Sidewinder.

Alternating between the comic and the sinister, fantasy and madness, Polynesian spirituality and European angst, *The Frigate Bird* is a powerful work by one of the Pacific's foremost writers.